A NOVEL BY
LIONEL WHITE

Black Mask Books
www.blackmask.com

THE KILLING
LIONEL WHITE

ISBN: 1-59654-574-7

BOOK DESIGN BY Goodloe Byron

BLACK MASK
AN IMPRINT OF DISRUPTIVE PUBLISHING, INC.

The Killing was originally published under the title *Clean Break.*

THE KILLING

⁂CHAPTER I⁂

The aggressive determination on his long, bony face was in sharp contrast to the short, small-boned body which he used as a wedge to shoulder his way slowly through the hurrying crowd of stragglers rushing through the wide doors to the grandstand.

Marvin Unger was only vaguely aware of the emotionally pitched voice coming over the public address system. He was very alert to everything taking place around him, but he didn't need to hear that voice to know what was happening. The sudden roar of the thousands out there in the hot, yellow, afternoon sunlight made it quite clear. They were off in the fourth race.

Unconsciously his right hand tightened around the thick packet of tickets he had buried in the side pocket of his linen jacket. The tension was purely automatic. Of the hundred thousand and more persons at the track that afternoon, he alone felt no thrill as the twelve thoroughbreds left the post for the big race of the day.

Turning into the abruptly deserted lobby of the clubhouse, his tight mouth relaxed in a wry smile. He would, in any case, cash a winning ticket. He had a ten dollar win bet on every horse in the race.

In the course of his thirty-seven years, Unger had been at a track less than half a dozen times. He was totally disinterested in horse racing; in fact, had never gambled at all. He had a neat, orderly mind, a very clear sense of logic and an inbred aversion to all "sporting events." He considered gambling not only stupid, but strictly a losing proposition. Fifteen years as a court stenographer had given him frequent opportunity to see what usually happened when men place their faith in luck in opposition to definitely established mathematical odds.

He didn't look up at the large electric tote board over the soft drink stand, the board which showed the final change in odds as the horses broke from the starting gate and raced down the long straight stretch in front of the clubhouse, on the first lap of the mile and a half classic.

Passing down the almost endless line of deserted pay-off windows, waiting like silent sentinels for the impatient queues of holders of the lucky tickets, Unger continued toward the open bar at the end of the clubhouse. He walked at a normal pace and kept his sharp, observant eyes straight ahead. He didn't want to appear conspicuous. Although Clay had told him the Pinkerton men would be out in the stands during the running of each race, he took no chances. One could never tell.

When he reached the bar and saw the big heavy-set man with the shock of white hair, standing alone at one end, he shook his head almost imperceptibly. He had expected him to be there; Clay had said he would. But still and all, he experienced an odd sense of surprise. It was strange, that after four years, Clay should have known.

The others, the three apron clad bartenders and the cashier who had left his box at the center of the long bar, stood in a small tight group at the end, near the opened doors leading out to the stands. They were straining to hear the words coming over the loud-speaker as the announcer followed the race.

There was a towel in the ham-like hand of the big man who stood alone and he was casually wiping up the bar and putting empty and half empty glasses in the stainless steel sink under it.

Unger stopped directly in front of him. He took the scratch sheet from his coat pocket and laid it on the damp counter, and then leaned on it with one elbow. The big man looked up at him, his wide, flat face carefully devoid of all expression.

"I would like a bottle of Heineken's," Unger said in his cool, precise voice.

"No Heineken's." The voice grated like a steel file, but also contained a gruff, good-natured undertone. "Can give you Miller's or Bud."

Unger nodded.

"Miller's," he said.

When the bottle and glass was placed in front of him, the bartender spoke, casually.

"Favorite broke bad—could be anybody's race."

"It could be," Unger said.

The big man leaned forward so that his paunch leaned heavily against the thick wide mahogany separating them. He kept his voice low and spoke in a conversational tone.

"He's in the ten win window, third one down, next to the six dollar combination."

Unger, when he answered, spoke in a slightly louder tone than was necessary.

"It is a big crowd," he said.

He drank half his beer and turned away.

This whole thing, this extreme caution on Clay's part, was beginning to strike him as a little foolish. Clay was playing it much too cagey. The man must have some sort of definite anxiety complex. Well, he supposed that was natural enough. Four years in state's prison would tend to make him a trifle neurotic.

The studiously hysterical voice of the announcer came alive in a high, intense pitch of excitement, but at once the context of his words was lost as the roar of the vast crowd swelled and penetrated the amphitheater of the all but deserted clubhouse.

Over and above the anonymous thunder of the onlookers, isolated, frenzied cries and sharp, wild islands of laughter reached the little man's ears. Too, there was the usual undercurrent of groans and the reverberations of thousands of stamping feet. And then there was the din as a terrific cheer went up.

Unger made his way, unhurriedly, once more toward the wide

doors leading to the stands.

With definite interest, but no sense of expectancy, his eyes went to the tote board in the center of the infield. Number eight had been posted as the winner. The red letters of the photo-finish sign showed for second place. As the horses which had reached the neighborhood of the third pole slowed to a halt and turned back toward the finish line, Marvin Unger shrugged and turned to re-enter the clubhouse. He went at once to the men's room, hurrying in ahead of the crowd.

Placing a dime in the slot, he entered a private toilet. He sat on the closed seat and took the handful of pasteboards from his pocket. Quickly he found the ticket on the number eight horse. He placed it on top of the others and then, removing his fountain pen from the breast pocket of his jacket, he carefully wrote on the margin of the ticket.

It took him not more than twenty seconds.

Getting to his feet, he tore the remaining tickets in two and scattered them on the floor. He then left the booth. He hadn't waited, outside there in the grandstand, to see what price the number eight horse paid. He had used his own money to place his bets, and although he was ordinarily an extremely prudent man as far as financial matters were concerned, he really wasn't interested. Irrespective of what the horse paid off, it must be considered a negligible sum.

After all, a few dollars could mean very little to a man who was thinking in terms of vastly larger amounts. A man who was thinking in the neighborhood of say a million to two million.

Moving toward the rapidly forming lines at the pay-off windows, Unger thought again of Clay. He wished that it was Clay himself who was doing this. But then, in all fairness, he had to admit that Clay had been right. It would have been far too risky for him to have appeared at the track. Fresh out of prison after doing that stretch and on probation even now, he would almost be sure to be recognized.

As a small cog in the metropolitan judicial system, Marvin Unger had a great deal of respect for the forces of law and order. He knew only too well the precautions Clay would have to take. His appearance, and recognition, at the track would be more than sufficient to put him back behind bars as a parole violator.

Unger once more reflected that Clay was unusually cautious. However, that element of caution in the man's character was all for the best. Even this more or less cloak and dagger method of making the initial contacts might prove to be the safest plan. They couldn't be too careful.

Regardless of the logic of his reasoning, he still resented being the instrument used. He would have preferred that the other man assume the risks.

He found a place behind a large, perspiring woman in a crumpled print dress, who fanned herself futilely with a half dozen yellow tickets, as the long line slowly moved toward the grilled window. It was the ten dollar pay-off window, the third one, and the one next to the six dollar combination.

The fat woman had made a mistake and she was told to take her tickets, which were two dollar tickets, to another window. She protested but the cashier, in a tired and bored voice, finally straightened her out. The annoyance of having to start all over at the end of another long line, however, failed to wipe the good-natured expression from her heavy face. She was still very happy that she had picked the winner.

Unger looked up at the face of the man behind the iron grill-work as he pushed his single win ticket across the counter. The ticket was faced down.

Without apparently observing him, the man's hand reached for the ticket and he turned it over and looked at it for just a second. Expressionless, he tore off one corner and then carefully compared it with the master ticket under the rubber at his right. As he did so he memorized the writing which Unger had put on the ticket in the men's room.

His face was still completely without expression as he read: "712 East 31st Street room 411 8 o'clock."

A moment later he tossed the ticket into a wicker basket under the counter and his lean, agile fingers leafed through several bills.

"Fifty-eight twenty," he said in a monotonous voice, shoving the money under the grill.

For the first time he looked up at Unger and he was unable to completely conceal the glint of curiosity in his faded, gray-blue eyes. But he gave no other sign.

Unger took the money and carefully put it in his trouser pocket before turning away from the window.

Clay is being overcautious, he thought, as he went out through the clubhouse and into the stands. It would have been safe enough for that bloated, red-faced Irishman back of the bar to have given the man the address. However, Clay had insisted that he knew what he was doing. He wanted to take no chances at all.

Marvin Unger remembered Clay's words when he, Marvin, had protested that the whole thing had seemed far too complicated.

"You don't know race tracks," he had said. "Everybody is watched, the bartenders, the waiters, the cleanup men—everybody. Particularly the cashiers. It will be dangerous enough to have us all get together in town—we can't take any chances of arousing suspicion by having Big Mike and Peatty seen talking together at the track."

Well, at least it was arranged. Peatty had the address now and Big Mike also had it. It had been written on the edge of the scratch sheet which Unger had left on the bar when he had finished his beer.

Unconsciously he belched and the thin corners of his mouth tightened at once in annoyance. He didn't like beer; in fact he very rarely drank at all.

Unger sat far back in the grandstands during the rest of the day's card. He made no other bets. A quick mental calculation informed him that he was already out approximately sixty dollars or more as a result of his activities. It bothered him and he couldn't help resenting the expenditure. It was a lot of money to throw away for a man who made slightly less than five thousand a year. It was a damned nuisance, he thought, that Clay lacked the money to finance the thing himself. On the other hand, he had to admit that had Clay possessed the necessary capital, he, Marvin Unger, would never have been taken in on the deal.

He shrugged it off and stopped thinking about it. What, indeed, would a few hundred or a couple of thousand mean in comparison to the vast sum of money which was involved? His final thought on the subject was that he was lucky in at least one respect—he might have to put up the expenses but at least he wouldn't have to be in on the violence. He wouldn't have to face the gunfire which would almost be sure to take place when the plan was ultimately consummated.

His naturally aggressive personality, the normal complement of small stature and the inferiority complex he suffered as the result of an avocation which he considered far beneath his natural intellectual abilities, didn't encompass the characteristic of unusual physical courage. His aggressiveness was largely a matter of a deep-seated distaste for his fellow man and a sneering condescension toward their activities and pastimes.

Waiting stolidly until the end of the last race, Marvin Unger joined the thousands rushing pell-mell from the track to crowd into the special trains which carried the winners and losers alike back from Long Island to Manhattan.

He reached his furnished rooms on Thirty-first Street, on the fourth floor of the small apartment house, shortly after seven o'clock, having stopped off first for dinner.

* * * * *

Michael Aloysious Henty was exceptionally busy for the first twenty minutes after the finish of the last race. The usual winners stood five and six deep, calling for Scotch and rye and Bourbon and anxious to get in a last drink or two before joining the lines in front of the pay-off windows. The excitement of having won was still in them and the talk was loud and boisterous. A few of the last minute customers, however, leaned against the bar and morosely tore their losing tickets into tiny fragments before scattering them to the floor where they joined the tens of thousands of other discarded pasteboards which had been disgustedly thrown away by those without the foresight to select the winning horse.

Big Mike always hated this last half hour of his job. There was far too much work for the four of them and then there was always the argument with the half dozen or so customers who wished to linger on past closing time. Even after the final drink had been served, there was the bar to be cleaned up, the glasses to be washed and the endless chores of getting the place in order. Invariably the bartenders missed the last special train of the day and would have to wait an extra twenty or twenty-five minutes to get a regularly scheduled train back to New York.

Mike was always in a hurry to get on that train. He was an inveterate gambler and in spite of endless years of consistently losing more than half of his weekly pay check on the horses, he still had a great deal of difficulty knowing just where he stood at the close of the last race. He had no mind for figures at all.

Of course, as an employee of the track—or at least of the concessionaire who had the bar franchise at the track—he wasn't allowed to make bets at the regular windows. Instead, each night he would dope the following day's events and then in the morning, on his way to work, he'd drop off at the bookie's and place his bets. A solid, dependable man in spite of his weakness for the horses, he was given credit by his bookmaker and usually settled up at the end of the week when he received his salary check.

It was during the long train ride home that he would take out his scratch sheet and start figuring out how he had made out on the day. On this particular day, he was more than normally anxious to begin figuring. Because of what happened—of Clay getting in touch with him and the excitement and everything—he had been a little too optimistic and bet a good deal heavier than usual.

He knew that he had lost on the day, but he wasn't quite sure how much. Not only had he a poor mind for figures, but he couldn't remember pay-off prices from one minute to the next. He was only sure of one thing; he had bet a total of well over two hundred dollars on the afternoon's races and only one of his horses had come in.

There was a deep frown on his smooth forehead as he thought about it. And then, oddly enough, the same fragment of a thought passed through his mind which had passed through that of Marvin Unger.

What the hell was a few dollars, after all, in comparison to the hundreds of thousands which had preoccupied his mind these last few days?

Big Mike was suddenly aware of a commotion at the end of the bar and he looked down to see a tall slender girl who couldn't have been more than nineteen or twenty, laughing hysterically. The girl screamed something to her companion, a fat, middle-aged man with a bald perspiring head, and then, with a snake-like movement, she lifted the tall glass in her hand and dumped the contents down the front of the man's gaily flowered sport shirt.

Two of the other boys were already straightening things out and a private track policeman was rapidly moving toward the group, so Mike turned back to the work in front of him.

There was a look of stern reproach on his wide, flat face. Big Mike was a moral and straight-laced man, in spite of a weakness for playing the horses and an even greater weakness for over excess in eating. Sixty years old, a good Catholic and the father of a teen-aged daughter, he highly disapproved of the younger generation. Particularly that segment of it he saw each day lined up at the bar in front of himself.

Automatically he picked up a handful of used glasses from the bar and went back to thinking of money. Once more he thought of that vast sum—a million, perhaps even two million dollars. And then, from the money, his mind went to Johnny Clay.

Johnny Clay was a good boy. In spite of the four years in prison, in spite of his criminal record and everything else, Johnny was still a good boy. Mike's vanity had been very pleased when Johnny had remembered him from the old days and had looked him up, once he was out of prison and back in circulation.

Big Mike had known Johnny from the time he was a towheaded kid on the Avenue, when Mike himself was behind the stick at Costello's old bar and grill. Even in those days, when he had been still in knee pants, Johnny had been wild. But his heart had always been in the right place. He'd been smart, too. A natural-born leader.

Mike remembered him later, when he'd begun to hang around the bar and play the juke box. He'd never been a fresh kid and he drank very little. He'd never given Mike any trouble at all.

Of course Big Mike hadn't approved of the way Johnny got by. There was no doubt but what he'd been on the wrong side of the law. And Mike had been pretty upset when the cops had finally picked up young Johnny and put him away on that robbery rap.

It was only in recent years that Mike had become a little more liberal in his thinking. The endless poverty of his life and his constant struggle to get along on a bartender's salary—a salary which he invariably shared with a series of bookmakers—had embittered and soured him. When he thought of all that money which went through the grilled windows of the track every day, he began to wonder if there would be really anything wrong in diverting some of it in his own direction.

He had thought about it often enough, God knows. But it was only when Johnny got out and had approached him with the idea that the thought was anything but an idle daydream. Well, if anything could be done about it, he reflected, Johnny was certainly the boy to do it. That night he'd know a lot more about the whole thing. He tried then to remember the address which had been written on the side of the scratch sheet the man had left at the bar. He couldn't remember it, but the fact didn't worry him. He had the sheet in his coat pocket.

He did remember that the time had been set for eight o'clock.

He'd have to hurry through his dinner to make it. Mary would be annoyed that he was going out for the evening. He had promised her he would talk with Patti.

A worried frown crossed his heavy face as he thought of the girl. Lord, it seemed like only yesterday that she was a long-legged baby in bobby socks, her flaming red hair done up in two stringy braids.

Patti was a good girl, in spite of what her mother, Mary, said. It was the neighborhood, that was the trouble.

Money, money to get away from the Avenue and out into the country some place. That's all that was needed.

Mike would like to move himself. He hated that long train ride from New York to the race track and back each day. Yes, a small, modest little house with a garden, somewhere out past Jamaica—that would be the ticket. It began to look as though the old dream might really come true.

By the time the Long Island train was roaring through the tunnels under the East River, Mike had figured out that he'd lost a hundred and twenty-two dollars on the day. His furrowed forehead was pale and beads of sweat stood out on it. A hundred and twenty-two dollars—Jesus, it was a lot of money. Almost half what he had promised to get together for Patti so that she could take that stenographic course at the business college.

Big Mike got to his feet while the train ground to a stop at Penn Station.

What the hell, he thought, another month and he could be giving that kind of money away for tips. He was one of the first ones out of the car; he was in a hurry. He had a lot to do before eight o'clock that night and he didn't want to be late.

*****

George Peatty caught the same train which had taken Big Mike back to Manhattan. He had even seen Mike, ahead of him in the small crowd at the station, but he had made no effort to reach the bartender's side. He had known the other man for a number of years, but they were only acquaintances—not friends. This, in spite of the fact that Mike had been responsible in a way for getting him his job at the track.

It wasn't that they didn't like each other; it was merely that they had nothing in common. Nothing, that is, except George's mother, who had been a girlhood friend of Mary McManus, who later became Mary Henty, Mike's wife. But George's mother was dead and it had been all of ten years since she had induced her friend Mary to intercede with Big Mike in order to get her son an introduction to one of the track officials.

George had, of course, been duly grateful. But it had ended there. George had always felt a sense of embarrassment with the older man. Big Mike had known a little too much about him; had known about the early days when George was pretty wild. He had had a bad reputation for getting into scraps.

But that had all been a long time ago; long before he'd met Sherry and fallen in love with her.

Watching Big Mike enter the train, George turned and walked down the side of the car until he came to a second car. He climbed aboard and found a seat well to the rear.

At thirty-eight, George Peatty was a gaunt, nervous man, who looked his age. His brown eyes beneath the receding line of thin, mouse-colored hair, had a tendency to bulge. His nose was large and aquiline and he had a narrow upper lip which unfortunately failed to conceal his crooked, squirrel-like teeth. His chin was pointed and fell in an almost straight line to his overlarge Adam's apple.

He had the long fingered hands of a pianist and kept them scrupulously clean. His clothes were conservative both as to line and price.

The moment he was seated, he unfolded the evening paper which he had picked up at the station newsstand. He started to read the headlines and his eyes remained on the page, but in a second his mind was far away. His mind was on Sherry.

After two years of marriage he still spent most of his idle time thinking of his wife. He was probably, now, more obsessed than he had ever been, even in the very beginning.

George Peatty's feeling toward his wife had never changed since the day when he had first met her, some year and a half before they were married. He loved her, and was in love with her, but even beyond that, he was still wildly infatuated with her. Marriage had served only to intensify the depth of his passion. He had never recovered from his utter sense of bewilderment when she had finally agreed to share his bed and his life. He still believed that he was the luckiest guy in the world; notwithstanding the fact that he fully realized that he was far from being happy. Luck and happiness were, for him, two completely different things, although he recognized that in his case they were the reverse sides of the same coin.

Thinking of Sherry, he began, as he always did on the train ride back to his apartment on the upper West side, a silent prayer that Sherry would be there when he got home. As a man who had spent years unconsciously figuring odds, he knew automatically that the chances were about one in ten that she would be.

The heavy vein in the right side of his neck began to throb and there was a nervous tick at the corner of his eye as he thought about it. As crazy as George Peatty was about his wife, he was not completely blinded to her character or to her habits. He knew that she was bored and discontented. He knew that he himself, somehow along the way, had failed as a husband and failed as a man.

In the hard core of his mind, he blamed the thing not on himself and certainly not on Sherry. He blamed it on luck and on fate. A fate which limited his earning capacity to what he could make as a cashier at the track. A fate which had made Sherry the sort of woman she was—a woman who wanted everything and everything the best.

Not, George thought, that she didn't deserve everything. Anyone as lovely as Sherry should be automatically entitled to the best that there was.

Dropping the newspaper in his lap, he closed his eyes and leaned his head back. He was suddenly relaxed. It wouldn't be long. No, it wouldn't be long before he would be able to give her the things which she wanted and deserved.

His lips moved slightly, but wordlessly, as he said the words in his mind.

"Thank God for Johnny."

At the moment he was only sorry about one thing. He would have liked to have told Sherry about the meeting he was going to at eight o'clock that night. He would have liked to have told her about the entire thing. Even now he could see her smoldering eyes light up as he would outline it to her.

But then, almost at once, he again began to worry about whether or not she'd be home.

Getting off at the station in New York, he stopped at a florist shop in the Pennsylvania arcade and bought a half dozen pink roses before getting into the subway and taking the express up to a Hundred and Tenth Street.

* * * * *

Looking down at the shock proof silver watch on his large wrist, Officer Kennan noticed that it was twenty-two minutes before six. Carelessly he swung the wheel of the green and white patrol car and turned into Eighth Avenue. He would just have time to drop by Ed's for a minute before taking the car into the precinct garage and checking out for the day.

Time for two quick ones and a word or two with Ed and then he'd be through for twenty-four hours. God, with the traffic the way it was in New York these days, he could sure use the rest. It was murder. He was not only thirsty but he was thirsty for a couple of good stiff shots. Thinking about Ed's he began to worry about the chances of running into Leo. Christ but he hoped that Leo wouldn't be around. He was into him now for well over twenty-six hundred dollars and he hadn't made a payment in more than three weeks.

Not that Leo really worried him; he would be quick enough to tell the little bastard where to get off. The only thing was that Leo had connections. Important connections with some of the big brass in the department. That was one reason Leo had not hesitated to loan him money when he needed it. It was the reason Leo confined the bigger part of his loan shark business to cops and firemen. He had political pull.

For a moment Randy Kennan, patrolman first class, considered the possibility of passing up Ed's. But once more he shrugged. He wanted those two drinks and Ed's was about the only place he knew where he could walk in and get them without trouble and without embarrassment. Also, without money.

He drove to Forty-eighth Street and turned east and went a half a block and then pulled over to the right hand side of the street. There was a mounted patrolman leaning over the neck of his horse, talking to a cab driver, not far from the corner. The street was crowded with traffic and hurrying pedestrians, but Officer Kennan didn't bother to pay them much attention.

He left the keys in the car and pulled up the brake as he opened the door. A moment later he walked several hundred feet down the street and turned into a bar and grill.

There were a couple of dozen customers lining the bar but Randy Kennan walked directly through to the back room. Ed saw him as he passed opposite the cash register and looked up with a nod and a friendly smile. Randy winked at him.

He liked Ed and Ed liked him. It wasn't like shaking a bartender down for a couple of fast shots. They were friends. Had been friends now for a good many years. In fact from the time they were kids together over at St. Christopher's.

He was about to push through the swinging doors into the kitchen when he heard his name called. He didn't have to look.

It was Leo and Leo was sitting where he usually sat, in the very last booth at the left. He was alone.

Randy hesitated a second and looked over at him. Then he sort of half nodded his head toward the kitchen door. He didn't want to go to the booth, even if Leo was alone. It would be bad enough if some passing lieutenant or captain wandered in, finding him there at all. It would never do to be found sitting in a booth in uniform.

There were two Italian chefs and a dishwasher in the kitchen but Randy gave them not the slightest attention. He walked over to a counter and picked up a slice of cheese from a plate. He was munching it a minute later when the swinging doors opened and Ed came in. He carried a bottle of rye in one hand and a glass in the other.

"Hot day, kid," he said as he sat them on the table next to Randy. "I see your pal Leo outside. He wants to talk to you."

Randy smiled at his friend, sourly.

"Tell the sonofabitch to come in here and talk," he said. "He knows damn well I can't..."

"I'll tell him, Randy," Ed said.

"How about joining me in one," Kennan said, looking up from the drink he was already pouring.

"Hell boy," Ed said, "I'm just coming on. You're going off, aren't you?"

Randy nodded.

"Yeah."

Ed left a half minute later to get back to the rush of customers. Leo passed him in the doorway.

Everything about Leo Steiner was bland. His soft brown eyes were almost childlike in their innocence; the large, un-wrinkled face was heavy with good nature and friendliness. He always spoke as though he were half laughing. Leo wore a nylon sports shirt with the top button fastened and no tie. He affected sports jackets and flannel trousers. There wasn't a thing about him which wasn't completely deceptive.

"Randy boy," he said. "How's tricks?"

Officer Kennan nodded in a noncommittal way. He indicated the bottle of whiskey with a nod of his head.

"Drink?" he asked.

"You know I never touch the stuff," Leo said and laughed as though it were a joke. "My nerves. It gets my nerves."

Randy smiled wryly. Nerves? Hell, Leo Steiner had about as many nerves as a hippopotamus.

Leo leaned back against the table so that he half faced the other man.

"You know, kid," he said, "I'm in a little trouble. Maybe you can help me out."

Randy nodded again. Here it comes, he thought.

"Yeah," Leo said, looking anything but like a man in trouble. "It's money. Gotta raise some quick dough. What do you..."

"Look, Leo," Randy said. "You don't have to beat about the bush. I know I'm late and I know just what I owe you. But I gotta have a little more time. Things have been breaking bad lately. I need time."

"Boy," Leo said, "I know just how it is. I sure want to give you all the time in the world. But the trouble is, I just can't do it. I need to get up some cash and right away. Guess I'll have to get say around five notes from you this week."

Randy reached for a second drink and swallowed it hurriedly. He turned to the other man and spoke quickly.

"Leo," he said, "I can't do it. I just can't make it this week!"

"You get paid this week," Leo said.

"Yeah, I get paid. But I'm in hock to the pension fund for a loan and when they take out theirs, I got just about nothing left at all. I gotta have a little more time."

Leo shook his head, sadly.

"How much time, Randy?"

Randy looked directly at the other man and spoke slowly.

"Listen," he said. "I got something good coming up. Real good. But it takes time."

"What is it," Leo asked. "Not another horse, Randy?"

Kennan shook his head.

"No—not a horse. This is a sort of private deal. All I can tell you is, just give me say another thirty days, and I think I can take care of everything."

Leo nodded slowly.

"It's twenty-six hundred bucks now, Randy," he said. "All right, suppose we say another thirty days—let's say I can do that. And we'll call it an even three grand—thirty days from now."

Randy Kennan's eyes narrowed and there was a mean line around the corners of his mouth.

"Three grand—Jesus Christ! What kind of goddamned interest is that to ask a man."

"It's your idea, Randy," Leo said, his voice soft and almost sympathetic. "You want the thirty days—not me. I just want my money. In fact, Randy, I gotta go out now, on account you're not paying me anything, and borrow the dough. I gotta probably borrow it from my friend the Inspector—and you know how tight he is."

Kennan caught the full significance of the threat. He would have liked to grab the fat man by his lapels and slap him until he was silly. But he didn't dare. He knew what Leo could do; he knew Leo's connections.

"O.K." he said. "O.K. Shylock. Three grand in thirty days."

Leo reached over and patted the big man on the shoulder.

"Good boy," he said. "I know I can count on you, pal."

He turned and went back into the barroom.

Randy Kennan took a third drink. His hand was shaking and he gritted his teeth in anger as he poured from the bottle.

"The bastard! The fat bastard," he said under his breath.

Well, in thirty days he'd pay him. He'd pay the sonofabitch his three grand.

He began to dream of the future. He'd stay on the force for another six months, he figured, once it was all over and done with. Yeah, that would be the safest bet. But then, when things quieted down, he'd get out and get out fast. Someday, someday in the next few years he'd catch up with Leo. He smiled grimly when he thought of what he'd do to Leo Steiner.

He sat his glass down and looked again at his wrist watch. It was getting on and he'd have to hurry. He still had to turn in the patrol car, sign out and get showered and dressed in his street clothes. He wanted to find time to get something to eat, too, before he showed up for the eight o'clock appointment.

He was looking happier as he left Ed's place. He was thinking of that appointment.

It was luck, real luck. Running into Johnny like that, the very day he'd been sprung upstate, was the best thing that had ever happened to him. Yeah, that was the break he'd been waiting for for a long, long time now.

✳CHAPTER II✳

He's changed, she thought. Stretching out her slender, naked arm, she reached over to the night table at the side of the bed and fumbled around until she found the pack of cigarettes. She brought it over to herself and hunched up so that she was half sitting. She shook out a cigarette and then leaned over again to find the lighter. With the lights out, the room was only half dark as the mid afternoon sun filtered through the almost closed Venetian blinds.

She lit the cigarette and drew a deep lungful of smoke, slowly expelling it. Her eyes went to the man lying beside her. His own eyes were closed and he lay completely still, but she knew that he wasn't sleeping.

Once more she thought, he's changed. It was odd, but something about him was different. Physically, the four years hadn't seemed to have altered his appearance in the slightest. There was, of course, that new touch of gray over his ears. But he was still a lean, hard six feet one, his face still carried the sharp fine lines, his gray eyes were as clear and untroubled as they had always been. No, the change wasn't a physical one.

For that she was glad. She wouldn't have been able to stand it if those four years had done to him what they do to most men who go to jail and come out shattered and embittered.

Johnny had been right about one thing; he had done it on his ear. He'd taken the rap and put it away and he hadn't let it hurt him.

No, it wasn't a physical change. It was something far more subtle. Not that the time behind bars had soured him. It hadn't even taken that almost boyish optimism and wild enthusiasm from him.

He still talked the same and acted the same. He was still the same old Johnny. Except that in some way or another he seemed to have settled down. Now, there was a new, deep, serious undercurrent to him which hadn't been there before. A sort of grim purposefulness which he had always lacked.

It was as though he had finally grown up.

Her hand went across to him and she softly rubbed the side of his head. He didn't move and instinctively she leaned over and kissed him gently on the mouth.

God, she was just as crazy about him as she had always been. More so. She was glad now that she had waited.

Four years had been a long time, a hell of a long time. For a moment she wondered what those years might have done to her. But at once, she dismissed the thought. Whatever they had done, it hadn't seemed to bother Johnny at all. He was just as much in love with her as he had always been. Just as impetuous and just as demanding. It was one of the things which made her always want him and need him—his constant demand for her.

Twisting her lovely, long limbed body, she put her feet on the floor at the side of the bed and sat up.

"It's getting late, Johnny," she said. "Must be after four. I'll get dressed and make us a cup of coffee. You suppose this man has any coffee around the place?"

He opened his eyes wide then, and looked around at her. He smiled.

"Come on back," he said.

She shook her head and the shoulder length blonde hair covered the side of her face.

"Not on your life, baby," she said. "You get up now and get dressed. I want to be well out of here before this Unger character gets home."

He grunted.

"Guess you're right, honey. You hit the bathroom; I'll be up in a second. There's a coffeepot in the kitchen. See if you can find something for a couple of sandwiches."

He reached for a cigarette from the package she had replaced on the table. The girl stood up and crossed the room toward the bath. She reached and took a handful of clothes from the back of a chair as she passed. A moment later the door closed behind her.

Flicking an ash on the floor, he thought, God it was worth waiting for. Worth every bitter second of those four years.

When he heard the sound of the shower, he too got up. He pulled on his clothes carelessly and was tucking in his shirt as she once more returned to the room.

"Honey," he said, looking at her with the admiration still deep on his face, "honey, listen. The hell with the coffee. Run down to the corner and pick up a bottle of Scotch. Jesus, I feel like a drink. I want to celebrate. After four years, I feel like something a little stronger than coffee."

She looked at him silently for a second and then spoke.

"You sure it's a good idea—drinking?" she asked.

He smiled.

"You don't have to worry," he said. "Nobody ever had to worry about my drinking. It's just that I feel like celebrating."

"Well," she said, slowly, "all right, Johnny. You know what you want. The only thing is, remember, it's been four years and it's likely to hit you awful fast. You want to be wide awake for tonight."

He nodded, at once serious.

"I'll be wide awake," he said. "Don't worry—I'll be plenty wide awake."

She smiled then, and pulling on the little cardinal's hat, she sort of half shook her head to brush the hair back and turned toward the door.

"Be right back," she said.

"Wait," he said, "I'll get you some money."

"I've got money," she said and quickly opened the door and closed it behind her.

Johnny Clay frowned and sat in the straight-backed chair next to the window. He thought of the single five dollar bill which Marvin Unger had left him that morning—just in case. He laughed, not pleasantly.

"Tight bastard," he said, under his breath.

But at once his mind went back to Fay. Jesus, there was a million things he wanted to ask her. They hadn't hardly talked at all. There were so many things they had to tell each other. Four years is a long time to cover in a few minutes.

Of course he knew that she still had the job; that she still lived with her family out in Brooklyn. She hadn't had to tell him that she had waited for him and only him all these years. That he knew, unasked. Her actions alone had told him.

And he'd had damned little opportunity to tell her much. He'd only just briefly outlined his plans; told her what he had in mind.

He knew she wouldn't like the idea. Certainly she had felt bad enough about it that time, more than four years ago, when the court had passed sentence on him and he'd started up the river. And she'd always been after him to get an honest job, to settle down.

Yes, he'd been surprised when she hadn't started right in to make objections.

After he had told her about it, she'd been quiet for a long time. And then, at last, she'd said, "Well, Johnny, I guess you know what you're doing."

"I know," he'd told her. "I know all right. After all, I've had four years—four damned long years, to think about it. To plan it."

She'd nodded, looking at him with that melting look which always got him.

"Just be sure you're right about it, Johnny," she said. "Be awful sure you're right. It's robbery, Johnny. It's criminal. But you know that."

"I'm right."

There'd been no questions about the right or wrong of it.

That part she understood. Right now she was too happy in being with him, in loving him, to go into it.

"The only mistake I made before," he'd told her, "was shooting for peanuts. Four years taught me one thing if nothing else. Any time you take a chance on going to jail, you got to be sure that the rewards are worth the risk. They can send you away for a ten dollar heist just as quick as they can for a million dollar job."

But then, they hadn't talked any more. They had other things to do. More important things.

He had the ice cubes out and a couple of glasses on the table when she returned. She tossed her tiny hat on the bed and then sat on the edge of it as he fixed two highballs with whiskey, soda and ice. Silently they touched rims and then sipped the drinks.

Looking at him with a serious expression in her turquoise eyes, she said, "Johnny, why don't you get out of this place? It's depressing here; dingy."

He shook his head.

"It's the safest place," he said. "I have to stay here. Everything now depends on it."

She half shook her head.

"This man Unger," she said. "Just how..."

He interrupted her before she could finish the question.

"Unger isn't exactly a friend," he said. "He's a court stenographer down in Special Sessions. I've known him for a number of years, but not well. Then, at the time my case came up and I was sentenced, he looked me up while I was waiting to be transferred to Sing Sing. He wanted me to get a message through to a man who was doing time up there, in case I had a chance to do so. It turned out I did.

"When I got out I figured he sort of owed me a favor. I looked up his name in the phone book and called him. We got together and had dinner. I was looking around for a guy like him—a guy who'd be a respectable front, who had a little larceny in his heart and who might back the play. I felt him out. It didn't take long."

Fay looked at him, her eyes serious.

"Are you sure, Johnny," she asked, "that he isn't just playing you along for a sucker? A court stenographer..."

Johnny shook his head.

"No—I know just where he stands. The man isn't a crook in the normal sense of the word. But he's greedy and he's got larceny. I was careful with him and played him along gradually. He's all right. He went for the deal hook, line and sinker. He's letting me lay low here, he's making my contacts, arranging a lot of the details. He's going to cut in for a good chunk of the dough, once we get it. He won't, of course, be in on the actual caper itself. But he's valuable, very valuable."

Fay still looked a little doubtful.

"The others," she said, "they all seem sort of queer."

"That's the beauty of this thing," Johnny told her. "I'm avoiding the one mistake most thieves make. They always tie up with other thieves. These men, the ones who are in on the deal with me—none of them are professional crooks. They all have jobs, they all live seemingly decent, normal lives. But they all have money problems and they all have larceny in them. No, you don't have to worry. This thing is going to be foolproof."

Fay nodded her blonde head.

"I wish there was something I could do, Johnny," she said.

Johnny Clay looked at her sharply and shook his head.

"Not for a million," he said. "You're staying strictly out of this. It was even risky—dangerous—for me to let you come up here today. I don't want you tied in in any possible way."

"Yes, but..."

He stood up and went to her and put his arms around her slender waist. He kissed the soft spot just under her chin.

"Honey," he said, "when it's over and done with, you'll be in it up to your neck. We'll be lamming together, baby, after all. But until it's done, until I have the dough, I want you out. It's the only way."

"If there was only something..."

"There's plenty you can do," he again interrupted. "Get that birth certificate of your brother's. Get a reservation for those plane tickets. Begin to spread the story around your office about planning to get married and give them notice. You got plenty to do."

He looked over at the cheap alarm clock on the dresser.

"And in the meantime," he said, "you better get moving. I don't want to take any chances on Unger walking in and finding you here."

She stood up then and put her second drink down without tasting it.

"All right, Johnny," she said. "Only—only when am I going to see you again?"

He looked at her for a long moment while he thought. He hated to have her leave; he hated the idea that he couldn't go with her, then and there.

"I'll call you," he said. "As soon as I can, I'll call. It will be at your office, sometime during the first part of the week."

They stood facing each other for a moment and then suddenly she was in his arms. Her hands held the back of his head as she pressed against him and her half opened mouth found his.

She left the room then, two minutes later, without speaking.

* * * * *

It was exactly six forty-five when George Peatty climbed the high stoop of the brownstone front up on West a Hundred and Tenth Street. He took the key from his trouser pocket, inserted it and twisted the doorknob. He climbed two flights of carpeted stairs and opened the door at the right. Entering his apartment, he carefully removed his light felt hat, laid it on the small table in the hall and then went into the living room. He still carried the half dozen roses wrapped up in the green papered cornucopia.

About to open his mouth and call out, he was suddenly interrupted by the sound of a crash coming from the bedroom. A moment later he heard laughter. He passed through the living room and down the hallway to the bedroom. He wasn't alarmed.

Bill Malcolm was down on his knees on the floor, at the end of the big double bed, beginning to pick up the pieces of broken glass. The uncapped gin bottle was still in his right hand, carried at a dangerous angle. He had a foolish grin on his handsome face and George knew at once that he was drunk.

Betty, Malcolm's short, chubby wife, sat on the side of the bed. She was laughing.

Sherry was over by the window, fooling with one of the dials on the portable radio. There was a cigarette between her perfect red lips and she held a partly filled glass in her hand. She was dressed in a thin, diaphanous dressing gown and her crimson nailed feet were bare.

Instinctively, George knew that she was sober—no matter how much she may have had to drink. She looked up the moment George reached the door, sensing his presence.

"My God, George," she said, "take the bottle out of Bill's hand before he spills that too. The dope is drunk."

"He's always drunk," Betty said. She stood up and weaved slightly as she moved toward her husband.

"Come on, Bill," she said, her voice husky. "Gotta go." She reached over and took the bottle and put it down on the floor. "My God, you're a clumsy..."

"Oh, stay and have another," Sherry said. "George, get a couple more glasses..."

Bill reached his feet, wobbling.

"Nope," he said, thickly. "Gotta go. Gotta go now." He lurched toward the door.

"Hiya, Georgie boy," he said as he passed Peatty. "Missed the damn party."

Betty followed him out of the room and a moment later they heard the slam of the outside door.

George Peatty turned to his wife.

"My God, Sherry," he said, "don't those two ever get sober?"

Even as he said the words, he knew he was doing the wrong

thing. He didn't want to argue with her and he knew that any criticism of the Malcolms, his wife's friends from downstairs, always led to a fight. It seemed that lately anything he said upset Sherry.

Sherry looked at her husband, the long, theatrical black lashes half closed over her smoldering eyes. Her body, small, beautifully molded, deceptively soft, moved with the grace of a cat as she went over to the bed and curled up on it.

At twenty-four, Sherry Peatty was a woman who positively exuded sex. There was a velvet texture to her dark olive skin; her face was almost Slavic in contour and she affected a tight, short hair cut which went far to set off the loveliness of her small, pert face.

"The Malcolms are all right," she said, her husky voice bored and detached. "At least they have a little life in them. What am I supposed to do—sit around here and vegetate all day?"

"Well..."

"Well my fanny," Sherry said, anger now moving into her tone. "We don't do anything. Nothing. A movie once a week. My God, I get tired of this kind of life. I get tired of never having money, never going anywhere, doing anything. It may be all right for you—you've had your fling."

Her mouth pouted and she looked as though she were about to cry.

George heard the words, but he wasn't paying attention to them. He was thinking that she was still the most desirable woman he had ever known. He was thinking that right now he'd like to go over and take her in his arms and make love to her.

He held the flowers out in a half conciliatory gesture.

Sherry took them and at once put them down unopened. She looked up at her husband. Her eyes were cold now and wide with resentment.

"This dump," she said. "I'm damned tired of it. I'm tired of not having things; not having the money to do things."

He went over and sat on the side of the bed and started to

put his arm around her. Quickly she brushed it away.

"Sherry," he said, "listen Sherry. In another week or so I'm going to have money. Real money. Thousands of dollars."

She looked at him then with sudden interest but a second later she turned away.

"Yeah." Her voice was heavy with sarcasm. "What—you got another sure thing at the track? Last time you had one it cost us two weeks' pay!"

For a long minute he looked at her. He knew he shouldn't say anything; he knew even one word would be dangerous. That if Johnny were to learn he had talked, he'd be out. That would be the very least he could expect. He could also be half beaten to death or even killed. But then again he looked over at Sherry and he was blinded to everything but his desire for her. That and the realization that he was losing her.

"Not a horse," he said. "Something a lot bigger than any horse. Something so big I don't even dare tell you about it."

She looked up at him then from under the long lashes with sudden curiosity. She reached over and her body pressed against his.

"Big?" she said. "If you're serious, if this isn't just another of your stories, then tell me. Tell me what it is."

Again he hesitated. But he felt her body pressing against his and he knew that he'd have to tell her sooner or later. She'd have to know sometime. Well, the hell with Johnny. The reason he was in on the thing anyway was because of Sherry and his fear of losing her.

"Sherry," he said, "I'll tell you, but you'll have to keep absolutely quiet about it. This is it—the real thing."

She was impatient and started to pull away from him.

"It's the track all right," he said, "but not what you think. I'm in with a mob—a mob that's going to knock over the track take."

For a moment she was utterly still, a small frown on her forehead. She pulled away then and looked at him, her eyes wide.

"What do you mean?" she said. "The track take—what do

you mean?"

His face was pale when he answered and the vein was throbbing again in his neck.

"That's right—the whole track take. We're going to knock over the office safe."

She stared at him as though he had suddenly lost his mind.

"For God's sake," she said. "George, are you hopped up? Are you crazy? Why my God..."

"I'm not crazy," he said. "I'm cold sober. I'm telling you—we're going to hijack the safe. We're meeting tonight to make the plans."

Still unbelieving, she asked, "Who's meeting? Who's we?"

He tightened then and his mouth was a straight contrary line.

"Gees, Sherry," he said, "that I can't tell you. I can only say this. I'm in on it and it's big. Just about the biggest thing that has ever been planned. We're..."

"The track," she said, still unbelieving. "You and your friends must be insane. Why, nobody's ever knocked off a whole race track. It can't be done. Good God, there's thousands of people—hundreds of cops... George, you should know—you work there."

He looked stubborn then when he spoke.

"It can be done," he said. "That's just the thing; that's the beauty of it. It hasn't been done or even tried and so nobody thinks it's possible. Not even the Pinkertons believe it could be worked. That's one reason it's going to work."

"You better get me a drink, George," Sherry suddenly said. "Get me a drink and tell me about it."

He stood up and retrieved the gin bottle from the floor. Going out to the kitchen, he mixed two Martinis. He wanted a couple of minutes to think. Already he was beginning to regret having told her. It wasn't that he didn't trust Sherry—he knew she'd keep her mouth shut all right. But he didn't want her worrying about the thing. And of course, Johnny was right. No one at all should know about it except the people involved. Even that was risky enough.

He reflected that even he didn't know exactly who was in on the plot. Well, he'd learn tonight—tonight at eight o'clock.

Carefully carrying the glasses, he started for the bedroom. He decided that he'd tell Sherry nothing more, nothing at all. He had to keep quiet, not only for his own protection, but for her protection as well. But he felt good about one thing. Sherry knew, now, that there was a chance they'd be coming into a big piece of money. She'd be happier. A lot happier. With money he could get her back; really back.

Before George Peatty left the house to take a subway downtown to keep his appointment, he took off his jacket and tie and went into the bathroom to wash up. While he was out of the room, Sherry crossed over to where he had carefully dropped his coat over the back of a chair. She made a quick, deft search through his pockets. She found the slip of paper on which he had scribbled the address down on East Thirty-first Street so that he would be sure not to forget it.

Quickly she memorized the few words and then put the paper back in his pocket.

She was back on the bed when he returned and she tolerated his long kiss and caress before he left.

★ ★ ★ ★ ★

Number 712 East Thirty-first Street was an old law tenement house which had been built shortly after the Civil War. Countless generations of refugees from the old world had been born, brought up and died in its dingy, unsanitary interior. Around 1936 the building had been officially condemned as a fire trap, although it had been unofficially recognized as one for several decades, and ultimately evacuated. A smart real estate operator picked up the property and making use of a lot of surplus war material purchased for almost nothing, he rebuilt the place into a more or less modern apartment house. The apartments were all the same, two rooms, a bath and a kitchenette. There were four to a floor and the five floors of the building were served by an automatic, self-service elevator. The facade of the building had been refinished and it looked respectable.

Rents went up from $25 a month to $70 and the new landlord had no difficulty at all in filling the place, what with the critical housing shortage. In spite of his improvements, however, the building remained pretty much of a fire trap and it also remained, to all intents and purposes, a tenement house.

Marvin Unger was one of the first to move into the structure.

Getting off the train from Long Island, Unger looked up at the clock over the information booth and saw that it was shortly before six. He decided against going directly to his apartment, and went over and bought an evening paper with the final stock market quotations and race results. Folding the paper and carrying it under his arm, he left the station and walked north until he came to a cafeteria. He entered and took a tray. Minutes later he found a deserted table toward the rear. He put his food down, carefully placed his hat on the chair next to himself and opened up the newspaper. He didn't bother to look at the race reports. He turned to the market page and began to check certain stock figures as he started to have his dinner.

At a time when almost every amateur speculator was making money on a rising market, Unger had somehow managed to lose money. A frugal man who lived by himself and had no expensive habits, he had saved his money religiously over the years. He invested the slender savings in stocks, but unfortunately, he never had the courage to hang on to a stock once he had bought it. As a result he was constantly buying and selling and, with each flurry of the market, he changed stocks and took losses on his brokerage fees. He also had an almost uncanny ability to select the very few stocks which went down soon after he bought them. Of the several thousand dollars he had managed to scrimp and put away from his small salary over the years, he had almost nothing left.

He finished his dinner and went back to the counter for a cup of coffee.

A few minutes later he started to walk across town in the

direction of his apartment. He passed a delicatessen on his way and stopped in. He ordered two ham and cheese sandwiches and a bottle of milk. For a moment he hesitated as he considered adding a piece of cake, but then he shook his head. What he had would be enough. There was no reason to pamper the man. God knows, this thing was costing him enough, both in time and in money, as it was.

The street door to the apartment house was unlocked, as it usually was until ten o'clock at night. He passed the row of mailboxes without stopping at his own. He never received mail at his residence and in fact, almost no one knew where he lived. He had not bothered to change the records down at the office giving his latest address the last time he had moved. He had an almost psychological tendency toward secrecy; even in things where it was completely unimportant.

He took the self-service elevator to the fourth floor and got out. A moment later he knocked gently on his own door.

Johnny Clay had a half filled glass in his hand when he opened the door.

Unger entered the dingy, sparsely furnished apartment and the first thing he noticed was the partly emptied bottle of Scotch sitting on the table in the small, square living room. He looked up at the other man sourly.

"Where'd you get the bottle?" he asked. At the same time he walked over and picked it up, reading the label.

Johnny frowned. The faint dislike he had felt for the other man from the very first was rapidly developing into a near hatred.

He resented the very fact that he was forced to stay in Unger's dismal, uncomfortable place; he hated his dependence on him. But at once he reflected that an out-and-out argument was one thing which must be avoided at all costs. He couldn't afford to fight.

"Don't worry," he said, avoiding a direct answer, "I don't get drunk. I just got tired of sitting around with nothing to do. Why the hell don't you get a television set in this place? There isn't even a book around to read."

Unger set the bottle back on the table.

"Was Sing Sing any pleasanter?" he asked, his voice nasty. "I asked where you got the bottle."

"God damn it, I went down to the corner and bought it," Johnny said. "Why—do you object?"

"It isn't a case of objecting," Unger said. "It's just that it was a risky thing to do. The reason we decided you'd stay here is because it's safe. But it's only safe if you stay inside. Don't forget—you're on parole, and right now you're disobeying the terms of the parole. The minute you moved and quit that job, you left yourself wide open to being picked up."

Johnny started to answer him, to call him on it, but then, a moment later, thought better of it.

"Look, Unger," he said, "let's you and me not get into any hassle. We got too much at stake. You're right, I shouldn't show myself. On the other hand, a guy can go nuts just hanging around. Anyway, I'm hungry and there's nothing around the place. You bring me anything?"

Unger handed him the bottle of milk and the sandwiches.

"Care for a drink?" Johnny asked.

Unger shook his head.

"Going to wash up," he said. He started for the bathroom.

Johnny took the brown paper bag containing the food into the kitchen. His eyes quickly went around to make sure that he had left no signs of Fay's having been in the place. He didn't want to have to explain Fay to anyone.

In fairness he had to admit that Unger was right. If the man believed that he had been out of the place, he had a right to squawk. But at the same time, he resented the other man and his attitude. Christ, if Unger wasn't so damned tight, he'd make it a little more attractive for Johnny to stay put.

Marvin Unger rolled up his sleeves and turned on the cold water faucet in the washbasin. He started to lean down to wash his face and abruptly stopped halfway. The bobby pin was lying next to the cake of soap where he couldn't possibly have missed it. His face was red with anger as he picked it up and looked at it for a long moment.

"The fool," he said. "The stupid fool."

He put the bobby pin in his pocket and decided to say nothing about it. He, as well as Johnny, realized that they could not afford to have an open rupture.

For the first time he began to regret that he'd gotten mixed up in the thing in the first place. If anything went wrong, he said to himself bitterly, it would only serve him right. Serve him right for getting mixed up with an ex-convict and his crazy plans.

Thinking of those plans, he began to visualize his share of the profits if the deal turned out successful. It would be a fabulous sum. A sum he would never be able to make working as a court stenographer.

He shrugged his shoulders then, almost philosophically. If he was going to make crooked money the least he could expect was to be mixed up with crooks. Anyway, it would be over and done with soon. Once he had his cut, he'd make a clean break. The hell with the rest of them; he didn't care what happened to them.

Where he'd be none of them would ever reach him. And it wouldn't matter too much if the cops got onto them and they were picked up and talked. By that time Marvin Unger would have found a safe haven and a new identity. By that time he would be set for the rest of his life.

He turned back to the living room, determined to make the best of things until it was over and done with.

Johnny was munching the last of a sandwich as Unger went over to the hard leather couch and sat down.

"Everything went all right," he said. "Got the message to both of them."

Johnny nodded.

"Good."

"To tell you the truth," Unger said, "I wasn't much impressed with the bartender. He looked soft. The other one, the cashier, didn't seem quite the type either."

"I didn't pick them because they're tough," Johnny said. "I picked them because they hold strategic jobs. This kind of a deal, you don't need strong arm mugs. You need brains."

"If they have brains what are they doing..."

"They're doing the same thing you are," Johnny said, foreseeing the question. "Earning peanuts."

Unger blushed.

"Well, I hope you're sure of them," he said.

"Look," Johnny said, "I know 'em both—well. Mike—that's the bartender, is completely reliable. He's been around for a long time. No record and a good reputation. But he wants money and he wants it bad. He's like you and me—he no longer cares where it comes from, just so he gets it. He can be counted on.

"The other one, Peatty, is a different proposition. Frankly, I wouldn't have picked him for this deal except for one thing. He happens to be a cashier at the track and he knows the routine. He knows how the dough is picked up after each race, where it is taken and what's done with it. We had to have a guy on the inside. George has no criminal record either—or he wouldn't be working at the track. He used to be pretty wild when he was a kid, but he never got into any serious trouble. He may be a little weak, but hell, that doesn't matter. After all, we already agreed on one thing. The big trick is to actually get away with the money. Once we're clear, once we have the dough, then it's every man for himself."

Unger nodded.

"Yes," he said, "every man for himself. How about the other one—the cop?"

"Randy Kennan? Randy's one guy we don't have to worry about at all. He's not too smart, but you can count on him. He's a horse player and a skirt chaser, he puts away plenty of liquor, but he's no lush. His record in the department is all right. But he needs money to keep up his vices. I've known Randy for a long time. We were brought up together. In spite of the rap I took, we're still friends. No, Randy's O.K. You won't have to give him a second thought."

Unger looked thoughtful.

"But a cop," he said. "Jesus Christ. You're sure there's no chance he's just playing along with some idea of turning rat and getting himself a nice promotion?"

"Not a chance in the world," Johnny said. "I know him too well..." He thought for a moment, then added, "It's possible, of course, the same as it's possible you could do the same thing. But it doesn't make sense. You wouldn't throw over a few hundred grand to get a four hundred dollar a year raise, would you?"

Unger didn't say anything.

"One thing," Johnny said, "I learned in prison is this. There isn't a professional criminal who isn't a rat. They all are. They'd turn in their best friend for a pack of butts—if they needed a cigarette. Get mixed up with real criminals and you're bound to mess up a deal. That's the main reason I think this caper has a good chance of working. Everybody involved, with the exception of myself, is a working stiff without a record and a fairly good rep. On this kind of a heist, the first thing the cops are going to look for is a gang of professionals. The only one with a record is myself. And I'm in it because it was my idea."

He looked over at the other man, his eyes cynical. "There is another thing, too," he added, "that I'll say about myself. I never hung out with crooks; I never got mixed up with them. I've never been tied in with a job anything like this one. I'd be the last guy on the books the law would think of after this thing is pulled."

"I hope so," Unger said. "I certainly hope so."

"You want to remember also," Johnny said. "Anyone of us crosses us up, he's in just as deep as the rest of us. It won't be a case of the testimony of a bunch of criminals which will involve him; it'll be the testimony of honest working stiffs. You can rest easy about the boys—the only chances we take in the whole thing is the actual execution of the job itself."

Marvin Unger nodded, his eyes thoughtful. He took a cigar out of his breast pocket and neatly clipped off the end and put it between his thin lips. He was striking the match when the knock came on the door.

Instinctively both men looked over at the alarm clock. The hands pointed to eight exactly.

❊CHAPTER III❊

For a full five minutes after she heard the outside door close, Sherry Peatty sat motionless on the bed. There was a thoughtful, speculative expression in her usually very pretty, but listless eyes. The index finger of her right hand played with the tip of her small right ear. At last she made up her mind. She was out of bed then, with a quick soundless movement, and she thrust her small feet into a pair of high heeled slippers and pulled a silk robe over her shoulders. She crossed the room and went down the hallway to the living room. She didn't have to look up the telephone number in the book.

The man who answered the phone said that Val wasn't in and asked who was calling. She told him her first name but it didn't seem to mean anything to him. He hadn't seen Val and he wasn't expecting him. Also he didn't know where he might be. Sherry used the telephone book then and tried a couple of bars and a cocktail lounge. Exasperated, she went back to the original number. She was about to dial it, when her own telephone rang suddenly from the box next to the table and she jumped, startled.

It was Val.

"You alone?"

She said at once that she was.

He told her he had just got the message that she had called. He wanted to know where George was.

"He's gone out," she said. "I've got to see you at once. Right away, Val."

"Something wrong?" the voice asked, lazy, almost disinterested.

"Listen," she said, "right away. Nothing wrong—just that I got to see you."

The man's voice was smooth, but still only half curious.

"I told you, honey," he said, "that until you're ready to leave that husband of yours, I don't want any part of anything. I don't want to get..."

"Listen," Sherry said, urgency making her speak swiftly. "You'll be interested. You'll be plenty interested. Where can I meet you, Val? How soon?"

There was a long silence and then he spoke.

"Make it in front of the Plaza, say at a quarter to eight. I'll drive by."

She said that she'd be there.

Back in her bedroom and sitting before the dressing table, she thought, God damn him, if it wasn't for George, he'd never dare treat me this way. Oddly enough, however, she didn't blame Val—she blamed it all on George.

The thing which had first intrigued her about Val Cannon had been his colossal indifference. A woman who had never had the slightest difficulty in attracting men, she had at once been intrigued by the tall, dark, rather ugly man. She'd met him through the Malcolms; had run into him a half dozen times at their apartment during the afternoons. He and Bill Malcolm had some sort of connection and the two of them frequently hung around during the day time and played the horses over the phone, getting the results on the radio.

The man's overwhelming casualness had first piqued her and then acted almost as a challenge.

It had finally happened one time when he had been alone in the Malcolms' place and she had knocked at the door. They'd had a drink or two and one thing had led to another. They'd ended up in bed together and she had been pleased to note that the careless attitude of studied indifference had rapidly changed. But it had only changed for that one afternoon.

Later, they'd met outside several times.

Val drove a Cadillac convertible; he dressed expensively and he was a fast man with a dollar. He never talked about himself, never told her what he did or how he made his living. She soon took it for granted that he was mixed up in some sort of racket or other.

They hung around cocktail lounges, occasionally went out to the track together—staying well away from George's window, of course. Once he had taken her to a bar up on Ninth Avenue, a dimly lighted, tough looking place. He'd told her that he owned a piece of it. From the looks of the men hanging around the booths and silently staring at her, she'd had the impression it was a sort of gang hangout. Val had given her the telephone number of the place and told her if she ever wanted to get in contact with him, to call him there and leave a message. Today had been the first time she'd called.

It would be the first time she'd seen him now in several weeks. In fact, since the night they'd spent together at the hotel. Val, that night, had made himself clear.

"It's like this, kid," he told her, "I like you. Like you a lot. But the trouble is, I'm liking you too damn much. I got no objections to laying some other guy's wife, but I do object to falling in love with another guy's doll. So from now on, I think it's going to be best if we just forget about things."

She'd tried to protest, to tell him that George, her husband, didn't mean anything to her; that in fact, she couldn't even stand to have him touch her any more.

"O.K.," Val had said. "Leave him then."

"And if I leave him, what then? Do we..."

He'd looked over at her, his eyes indifferent, almost cold.

"I'm not making bargains," he said softly. "Leave him and we'll see what happens. I'm not going to horse trade. You get rid of that bum you're married to; get yourself free and clear. Then you and I can start fresh."

She'd been furious, burned up. She'd wanted to spit on him

and curse him. But she was crazier than ever about him and he must have known the power he had over her. He hadn't moved an inch.

When they'd left the hotel the next morning, he'd dropped her off a few blocks from her apartment.

"Lemme hear from you," he'd said.

She knew what he had meant. Let me hear from you when you have left your husband.

She had, at last, made up her mind to leave George Peatty. Her decision came on the very afternoon that he had come home and broken down and told her about the plan to rob the race track.

The doorman at the Plaza eyed her suspiciously as she walked back and forth in front of the main entrance of the hotel. She looked down several times at the tiny wrist watch and she knew that she still had a couple of minutes to wait. The doorman had asked if he could call her a cab, but she had shaken her head.

She was standing still, tapping her foot in irritation, when the Cadillac pulled around the circle and stopped opposite her. She started for the car, but the doorman reached in front of her and opened the door handle. He tipped his hat as she got in.

"Damn it, Val," she said, "I wish you wouldn't make me meet you on the street like this. That damned flunky thought I was out on the town."

Val laughed.

"Where to, kid?" he asked.

"Any quiet spot where we can talk," she said.

He nodded and was silent for a time as he swung the car into the traffic heading across town.

"Decided to dump old George at last?" he finally asked.

She looked at him, a surge of sudden anger coming over her. But when she spoke, her voice was calm.

"Something more important than that, Val," she said. "That is, if you consider money—say a million or so—important."

He looked over at her quickly and whistled under his breath.

"We better find a quiet spot," he said softly.

Twenty minutes later they were seated in a table-high booth in an almost deserted Chinese restaurant on Upper Broadway. Canned music drifted from a speaker on the wall over their heads and drowned out the sound of their voices as they talked in low tones. Neither did more than toy with the dishes in front of them.

Val listened quietly as Sherry told him of her conversation with George.

For several seconds, after she was through, he sat silent and thoughtful. Finally he looked up.

"You mean," he said, "that your husband told you seriously that he and some mob are planning on knocking over the race track? I just can't believe it."

She looked at him, annoyed.

"You can believe it all right," she said. "George may be a fool—in fact he is—but he's no liar. Don't forget, he works at the track; he'd be the logical guy to use as a fingerman on the job."

Val whistled, under his breath.

"He's crazy," he said. "The guy's nuts. It can't be done."

"Yeah, that's what I told him," Sherry said. "But he said that it was going to be done—that the job was all set up. They got the mob and they got everything set."

"Who's in it with him? He can't be masterminding it alone, that's for sure. I thought you always told me this husband of yours was strictly a square?"

Sherry shook her head.

"You can't tell about George," she said. "For me—I believe him."

Val reached for the drink he had ordered and hadn't touched so far. He stared for a long time at the girl before speaking.

"Look," he said finally. "What's your angle in this? Why are you telling me about it? I should think..."

"I'm telling you for a couple of reasons," Sherry said, her eyes bright and hard. "Until I learned of this when George got home,

I was all set to leave him. I guess you know why I was leaving, too. But now things are changed. If this deal goes through—if by some miracle they do knock off the track—George will be in the chips. He'll have plenty."

Quickly Val interrupted her.

"That's all he needs, isn't it?" he said, his thin lips cynical.

"He'd still be George," Sherry said. "With it or without it, he'd still be George."

Val nodded.

"And you think, that let's say they do pull the job and that George gets his cut, maybe I could take it away from him?"

Sherry stared him straight in the face and didn't blush. She nodded her head slowly.

"Yes," she said. "I think you could."

There was a long interval of silence and they picked at their food. Neither was hungry.

"How about the others—any idea who they are? Any idea when this thing is to come off?" Val asked at last.

"Only this," Sherry said, reaching for her handbag, and taking out her lipstick to repair her face. "I know George is having a meeting with the mob tonight. While he was cleaning up in the bathroom, I went through his clothes. I found a slip of paper. It said, 712 East 31st Street Room 411 Eight o'clock.'"

"Address mean anything to you?"

"Nothing."

Val took a cigar from a thin leather case. He put it in his mouth but didn't light it. For a long time again he thought before speaking.

"Kid," he said at last, "I think we got something. If they're having a meeting tonight, the chances are they'll be making final plans. Most of the mob will be there. And they'll take plenty of time. This thing, if it's true, is a lot bigger than you think. You're interested in George's cut, but sweetheart, let me tell you something. George's cut will probably be peanuts compared with the total take."

Sherry looked up at him then, sudden surprise on her face.

"What we gotta know," Val continued, "is a little more about the over-all plan. You think George will tell you anything..."

"Not a chance," Sherry interrupted. "I could see that he was scared stiff that he'd talked as much as he did. I don't think I'll find out any more until it's over and done with. George is smart enough to know that my interest isn't in what he's going to pull, but only in the dough that it brings in."

Val smiled thinly and nodded.

"Probably right," he said. He watched her closely as he continued to speak. "What we got to know," he said, "is who's at that meeting on Thirty-first Street and what goes on during it."

"You mean..."

"I mean that one of us wants to get up there and get outside the door of that room and case the place."

Sherry nodded, hesitantly.

"You're the baby to do it," Val said. "If by any chance your husband does run into you—that he leaves early or something—why tell him you just didn't believe his story in the first place. Tell him the address fell out of his pocket when he took his coat off, that you read it and thought he might be two timing you."

Sherry laughed.

"George knows damn well I wouldn't care if he was," she said.

"So what if he does know. You're smart; you can handle it."

A half hour later they left the restaurant and Val drove downtown. He dropped Sherry at Thirty-fourth Street.

"Take a cab and get out a half a block from the place," he said. "I gotta couple of things to do, but I'll be in the neighborhood a little later. George comes out and if he's got anyone with him, I want to tail them. You see what you can find out, but be careful as hell. Don't be seen if you can help it. I won't plan to see you again tonight, but I'll stop by tomorrow around noon, as soon as George leaves for the track."

Sherry was stepping into a taxi as he pulled the Caddie away from the curb and turned back uptown.

* * * * *

Only Marvin Unger looked up at him, sharp and startled, when he finished speaking. Big Mike sat solidly on the couch, his legs spread and staring at a spot of floor between his large feet. Randy Kennan stretched out in a chair, fingers interlaced in back of his neck and his eyes closed. Peatty paced back and forth at one end of the room, nervously dropping ashes on the floor.

"You mean to say," Unger said, "that there are going to be three more guys in this? Three more guys and that we're not to even know who they are?" He sounded incredulous.

"That's right," Johnny Clay said.

Unger almost snorted.

"What the hell is this anyway," he snapped. "I don't get it. First, why three more; secondly, why don't we know who they are? Don't you trust..."

Johnny stood up suddenly and his face was hard. His voice was tense with anger as he answered.

"Listen," he said. "Let's get something straight. Right now! I'm running this show. All the way through. And to answer your last question first—yeah, I trust you fine. But I don't trust the three men I'm bringing in on the deal. If you guys don't know who they are, then you can be sure they won't know who you are. That make sense to you?"

He stopped for a moment then and looked at the others. No one said anything.

"These guys we got to have," he said then. "One of them I need for the job with the rifle. Somebody's got to handle that and I don't think any of you want to do it."

Once more he looked at them, one after the other. Once more no one answered him.

"I need a second guy for the rumble in the lobby," he said. "The third one runs interference for me when I leave that office. These men are not going to be in on the basic scheme. They're getting paid to perform certain definite duties at a certain definite time. They're not cutting in on the take. They will be paid a flat price to do a straight job."

Kennan opened his eyes and looked at Johnny. He winked, imperceptibly and so that the others didn't see it.

"Johnny's right, Unger," he said. "They don't know who we are, or what the deal is, so much the better. And if we don't know who they are, what's the difference. If you don't know something, you can't talk about it."

Big Mike grunted.

"We can trust Johnny to handle that end all right," he said.

Unger still didn't seem satisfied.

"If they don't know anything about the basic plan, about the job," he asked, "then why are they doing it? How do they know they're going to get paid if they don't know where the dough's coming from?"

"Simple," Johnny said. "These boys are straight hoods. They get paid in advance. Five grand for the guy with the rifle; twenty-five hundred apiece for each of the others."

This time they all looked up at Johnny, startled.

It was Marvin Unger, however, who spoke.

"Ten thousand dollars," he said, aghast. "Where in the hell are you..."

Johnny cut in quick.

"Yeah, ten grand," he said. "And cheap. For Christ sake, we're shooting for between a million and a half and two million dollars. What the hell are you doing, screaming about a lousy ten grand?"

For the first time George Peatty spoke up.

"It isn't that, Johnny," he said, "it's just that where are we going to get the ten grand from."

Johnny looked at him coldly.

"What the hell do I care where you get it from," he said caustically. "There are four of you—that's twenty-five hundred apiece. You'll just have to get it up."

Unger interrupted angrily.

"Fine," he said, "just get it up. So what about you—you going to get your share up too?"

Johnny went over to the couch and sat down before answering.

"Listen," he said, at last, his voice unhurried. "Let's get one thing straight. This is my caper; I'm setting it up, I'm doing the brain work and the planning. I'm the one who figured it out and got you guys together. I've worked four damned long years perfecting this thing. Also, I'm the guy who's taking the big chance when we pull the job. I'm the guy who goes in with the chopper under his arm.

"Each one of you is working; each one has a job. You got some sort of income, some sort of legit connections. So go to the banks if you got any dough; borrow from 'em if you haven't. Go to the loan sharks if you can't get it from the banks. It's the least you can do. We're shooting for real money; you can't be pikers if you want in on this deal."

He turned suddenly to Marvin Unger.

"You," he said, "what about you? You're supposed to be financing this thing. What the hell do you think you're in this for—a few lousy sandwiches, a flop for a couple of weeks and a messenger service that any kid could handle? You're too goddamn yellow to waltz in on the caper itself—the least you can do is get up some dough!"

Unger reddened and for a moment looked sheepish.

Kennan stood up and stretched.

"I'm not at all sure, Johnny," he said, "that I can get any dough. I'm head over..."

Big Mike and Peatty both started to talk at once, but Johnny interrupted them.

"All right," he said, "let's settle it this way. We'll bring in three more boys; cut 'em in on the total take that you guys are splitting. It's simple enough."

They began to protest all at once and Johnny suddenly pounded the table in front of him.

"For Christ sake, quiet down," he said. "You want everyone on the block to hear you?"

Unger spoke then as the others suddenly stopped talking.

"All right," he said. "I guess it's up to me. I'll raise the ten grand. Only thing is," he added petulantly, "I feel I should be reimbursed..."

Randy Kennan guffawed.

"Haw," he said. "Reimbursed! Brother, you're being reimbursed several hundred thousand dollars worth. However, once we pull this job and get the dough, I'm perfectly willing to see you get an extra ten off the top."

The others agreed and Johnny turned back to the rolled up drawing lying on the table.

"Well, that's that, then," he said. "I'll see that the contacts are made, that the three boys are arranged for. Just be sure I got the money to operate on. I'll need half of it by the first of this next week; the other half the day before the big race."

He reached down and picked up the roll of paper and carefully spread it out.

"This is rough," he said. "It's a drawing of the clubhouse and track as I remember it. Randy," he turned toward the cop, "you got to get me a damned good street map of the whole district. And you, George, I want you and Mike to go over this drawing with me careful as hell. I want to bring it completely up to date. Add or subtract even the slightest change which may have been made. Even if it's something as unimportant as the placing of a soda stand."

The four men in the room crowded around him looking down at the two foot square of paper he spread out. Randy Kennan pulled a tall piano lamp over and took the shade off so that they could see better.

The room was thick with smoke and Unger began to cough. He left the table and walked to the window and started to raise it. Johnny turned toward him at once.

"Goddamn it," he said, "keep that window closed. You want..."

"It only opens on a court," Unger said.

"I don't care, keep it closed." He turned back to the table.

He reached down with the yellow pencil in his right hand so that it traced a line from the section marked off "club house" to the main entrance gate.

"This," he began, and then his voice went suddenly silent. He lifted his head and listened intently. In a moment he looked up at the others who were staring at him. He started to speak again, but quickly whirled and took three swift steps across the room. His hand reached out and he turned the snap lock on the front door of the apartment and jerked it open.

There was a quick short cry and the sound of a sudden scuffle.

A minute later and he was back in the room.

He held the girl by both arms as he pulled her in with him. She started to scream again and one of his hands reached up and covered her mouth.

"Close that door!" He snapped out the command as he half carried the girl across the room.

Randy Kennan quickly kicked the door shut. Mike and Unger stood in the center of the room, motionless and speechless. George Peatty was completely white and he weaved on his feet. He looked as though he were about to faint.

Johnny took his right hand from over the girl's mouth and simultaneously his left hand shot out and his fist caught her flush on the chin. She sank back on the couch unconscious.

* * * * *

"Oh my God, Sherry!"

The four men took their eyes from the girl and stared at George Peatty as the words left his mouth.

Randy Kennan was the first to recover. He was across the room in a flash. He spoke as he pulled the blackjack from his hip pocket.

"You stupid, double-crossing, son of a bitch," he said. He lifted the blackjack.

George was still staring helplessly at his wife as the weapon descended across the front of his forehead. He fell slowly to the floor.

Johnny reached the cop as his foot started back to kick the fallen man.

"Hold it," he said. "Hold it, boy. Get the girl in the other room before she comes to. We'll bring this bastard around and find out what this is all about. And keep it as quiet as you can. We don't want a rumble."

Unger was looking pale and he went over to a chair and sat down, his eyes still on the girl. Big Mike looked at Peatty for a moment and then went into the kitchen. He came back with a glass of water and threw it into the fallen man's face.

"Whoever she is," he said, "George knows her. But he wasn't expecting her; he was as surprised as any of us."

Kennan had lifted Sherry's slight, unconscious form and carried her into the other room. He closed the door behind himself and was gone several minutes before he returned. He held a small pocketbook in his hand and was carrying a driver's license.

"Tied her up and gagged her," he said. "It's his wife."

Johnny and Mike between them had lifted George Peatty up and half sat him on the couch. He was still unconscious.

"Christ," Mike said, "you shouldn't of hit him so hard. You maybe fractured his skull."

Randy grunted.

"Wish I had," he said. "The bastard. But don't worry. I didn't. I know how to hit them safe."

"Well, let's get him so he can talk," Johnny said.

Unger looked up then.

"He's supposed to be your friend, Clay," he said, "how well..."

"I know him," Johnny said shortly. "Let's just get the story before we go off half cocked."

"He must have told her," Randy said. "The damn fool, he must have told her about the meet."

Peatty began to groan and a moment later his eyes opened.

He looked up then, dazed, for a second. His eyes cleared and he darted a glance around the room. They could see that he was looking for his wife.

Johnny reached down and grabbed him by the lapels of his coat.

"O.K., George," he said. "O.K., boy. Let's have it Quick!"

Peatty looked up at him, watery blue eyes wide with fear. "Jesus, Johnny," he said, "she must a followed me. She must have followed me here. Where…"

"She's in the other room," Johnny said. "Never mind about her. Just tell me; what have you told her—what does she know?"

"Nothing," George said, stuttering to get the words out. "I swear to God she don't know anything. She must have followed me."

He looked up and his eyes were wide and beseeching.

"Johnny—Johnny, don't hurt her. She's—well, she doesn't mean anything."

Mike walked over in front of them. He stared coldly at George.

"You give her this address?"

George shook his head violently.

"God no!" he said. "I never even…"

Randy got up and slapped his face hard.

"Shut up," he said. "God damn it, Johnny, this does it. If this bastard's been talking…"

"I haven't," Peatty said. "I swear I haven't. She followed me."

"How much do you suppose she heard?" Johnny said.

Randy and Mike both shrugged.

"Couldn't have heard too much," Randy said. "But that isn't the point. What was she doing at that door listening? Why did she come? That's what we got to find out."

Marvin Unger crossed the room and spoke to Johnny.

"You got to get her out of here," he said. "We can't have anything happen here."

Johnny sat down on the couch and thought for several minutes. Finally he looked up.

"All right," he said. "There's only one thing to do. First, get Peatty out. You Randy, take him home; stick with him. Don't let him out of your sight. Mike, you and Unger take a powder for a while. Go for a long walk. I'm going to find out what she was doing here; what she knows."

Peatty looked over at Johnny, his eyes wild.

"God," he said, "don't hurt her. Don't do anything to her!"

"I'll..."

Peatty interrupted him.

"Listen, Johnny," he said. "I had the address here written down. I know it was crazy, but I thought I might forget it. She probably found it and came here. Maybe she thought I was two-timing her or something. Yeah, that was probably it. It couldn't have anything to do with the..."

"Pipe down," Randy said, making a threatening gesture.

"I won't hurt her," Johnny said. "But George, get one thing straight. I'm not letting anything interfere with this job. I've planned it too long; there's too much at stake. Nothing is going to crap up this deal—you or your goddamned wife or anything else."

"She doesn't know anything. She..."

"I'll find out what she knows," Johnny said. "Get up now and go with Randy. Don't give him no trouble. You're telling the truth then you got nothing to worry about."

"Johnny," Peatty said. "Please don't..."

Johnny Clay looked at him coldly.

"I'm going to find out what she knows," he said. "If she knows too much then she's got to be cooled off until this thing is over. Someway she's got to be cooled."

"You can't do it to her here," Unger said hurriedly. "Jesus, Clay, you wouldn't..."

"You damned fool," he said, "I'm not going to kill her. But I am going to find out the score. If you're nervous, take a powder."

Big Mike reached over and his ham-like hand grabbed Peatty by the shoulder and he pulled him to his feet.

"I'll go along with Randy," he said. "We'll take George out for a ride around the park for an hour or an hour and a half. You go ahead and do what you have to do."

A moment later he pushed the other man in front of him through the door. Randy followed on their heels.

Unger waited until they were gone and then turned to Johnny.

"I'll go out for a while," he said. "I don't want to..."

"Go ahead," Johnny said.

He turned to the bedroom as the other man put his hat on.

"Don't let this throw you," he said, over his shoulder. "Peatty himself is all right. I know he's O.K. About the dame—well, we'll soon find out. When you're shooting for this kind of dough," he added, "you have to expect trouble. It never comes easy. And I'd just as soon have the trouble now as later."

Unger didn't answer. He didn't look happy as he left the apartment.

Johnny hesitated for a minute and then turned and went to the door and locked it after the other man. He looked over toward the bedroom door then for a minute, but instead of going in that direction, turned and went into the kitchen. He poured a stiff shot of Scotch in a water glass and downed it without a chaser.

Then he went to the bedroom.

She lay in a crumpled heap on the bed, her hands bound with a necktie at her back. Her feet were also tied and her short skirt was hitched up almost to her waist.

Johnny tried to keep his eyes from the soft bare flesh of her thighs as he approached. He leaned down and with one hand turned her over so that she lay on her back facing up at him.

Her huge midnight eyes were wide open and they stared into his own.

He reached under her head and untied the handkerchief gagging her mouth. There was a single drop of blood on her chin.

He felt around and behind her and found the knot binding her wrists.

Untying it, he said, "One God damn peep out of you and I'll knock your teeth down your pretty throat."

As he released her hands he looked once more into her face. He looked for the fear that he knew he would find there.

She was looking right at him. She was laughing.

❊CHAPTER IV❊

She lay there on the bed, curled up like a kitten. Irrelevantly, he wondered how the hell did George ever rate anything this pretty.

There were other things on his mind, plenty of other things. But for the moment all he could do was think of George Peatty and this dark, sulky girl who was his wife. It was easy enough to understand what Peatty saw in her; but what had she seen in him?

He shrugged. The hell with it.

She had stopped laughing now and was watching his face, wide-eyed.

"You have an interesting breath," she said, suddenly. "Is there any more of it around?"

"You're not only nosy—you're a comedian."

She didn't smile.

"No," she said, "I just feel like a drink. The way you all are acting, I could use one. Where's George?"

"George went out for a walk," he said. "You and I are going to have a little talk."

"I talk better with a drink in me," she said.

He stared at her for a minute.

"All right," he said, "I'll get you a drink. Stay just where you are."

"Why should I move," she said. "I like beds. Make it a straight shot with a water chaser."

He turned and left the room. When he came back with the bottle and the glasses, she hadn't moved. He poured two stiff shots, then went back for a couple of glasses of water. He handed her the drink and the chaser.

She gulped it in two swallows and held out the empty glasses after sipping the water. Her small face, puckered in distaste, made her look like a little girl who had just taken some unpleasant medicine.

Johnny Clay barely touched his own drink. He put the glasses on the floor, then went over and closed the bedroom door. He pulled a straight backed chair alongside the bed and sat astride it, leaning his arms over the back.

"All right," he said. "Let's have it. What did George tell you— what are you doing here?" His eyes were bleak as he looked at her.

"He told me he was going out on business. I didn't believe him and so I followed him to this place. I was outside the door trying to listen, when you opened it."

"And what did you hear?"

"Nothing."

He stood up then, kicked the chair back so that it fell over. He reached down and took her by both arms, half pulling her from the bed to her feet. He shook her as he would have shaken a rag doll.

"You lie," he said. "What did he tell you? What did you hear?"

She stood straight then, directly in front of him, staring into his face.

"Stop shaking me," she said, her voice low and husky. "Stop shaking me and maybe I can talk."

He still held her by the arms, his fingers making deep marks in her soft flesh. He looked at her without expression. For a brief second they held the tableau.

The movement was so swift he had no time to prepare himself. Her right leg bent and she brought it up, catching him in the groin.

He suddenly freed her arms, bent double.

She stepped back and sat on the edge of the bed.

"Don't manhandle me, you bastard," she said.

Gradually he straightened himself. His face was white with pain and anger.

"You bitch! You bitch, I could..."

"You could sit down and listen to me," she said. "And keep your hands off of me until I want you to touch me. I haven't done anything. It's like I told you, I followed George here. I was listening outside the door, but I couldn't hear anything. You think I'm lying, go outside and try it. You won't hear anything."

"Do you always follow your husband around?" Johnny asked.

She smiled.

"God no. He never, usually, goes anywhere. But he said it was business and I just wanted to know what kind of business. So maybe now that we're friends again, you can tell me."

"We're not friends," Johnny said.

"We could be. Very good friends." She stood up and walked toward him. "What's the matter?" she asked. "Aren't I your type?"

He stared at her. She's any man's type, he thought. He also realized he was getting nowhere. She wasn't the kind of girl to frighten. He suddenly knew that he'd never learn anything, trying to bully it out of her. It was an effort, because he was still in pain, but he smiled. It was the old Johnny smile, the smile which had always charmed them.

"Jesus," he said, "old George really took the jackpot."

She liked it.

"Think so?" she asked. "Maybe you're right—only I don't like that word pot."

"Come here," he said.

"Men come to me."

He took a step then and reached for her.

This time his hands didn't stop at her arms. He reached around her slender, trim waist, pulled her to him. One hand cupped in back of the tight dark curls as she lifted her small face.

She leaned close to him and her own hand went behind his head, pulling his face to her own.

Her mouth was moist and her lips half parted. She clung to him then and he felt the fire of her tongue.

He'd started it as a trick, a technique designed toward a definite end. It didn't stay that way.

He half carried her over to the bed.

In that next moment he tried to tell himself that this was business, strictly business. He had to find out what she knew and this was the best way to do it.

But he knew different. He knew that it was more than business; a lot more. He thought, then, in a flashing moment, of Fay, with whom he had shared this same bed just a few hours previously. Instinctively he hesitated, but just as instinctively, his muscles again tightened. And then, for the next few moments he was unable to think clearly of anything.

One hand was fumbling with the catch of her brassiere when it happened.

She was like an eel; one second she was in his arms, pushing against him, her lips still pressed to his own. And then in the next second she had wriggled free and darted across the room and stood over by the window.

She was laughing.

"Some guy," she said. "You work fast. Don't you think I should at least know your name?"

He sat on the edge of the bed and stared at her. It took him a half a minute to come to. And then he, too, laughed.

"You are right, Mrs. Peatty," he said. "You certainly should. I'm Johnny—Johnny Clay, a friend of your husband's."

She watched his face, still half laughing.

"I didn't know George had friends like you," she said. "Where's he been hiding you, anyway?"

"Where's he been hiding you?"

"He's been hiding me any place where I can't spend money,"

she said. "And that should answer your first question. George told me he had a date with a guy about a business deal which might lead to some real dough. That's all he told me. I'm interested in money—among other things. That's why I came; I wanted to know if he was telling the truth, or if it was just another one of his pipe dreams."

He nodded, slowly. He began to get the picture. Suddenly, he felt sorry for Peatty.

"How long have you and George been married?" he asked.

She sulked then, for a minute.

"It's really none of your damned business," she said. "But a couple of years. Too long, in any case. Let's get back to the point—what's the big business deal?"

"Didn't you hear?" he asked.

"I told you I just got to the door when you heard me. I didn't hear anything. If I had, I wouldn't have to ask. Anyway, you can tell me anything you can tell George. Whatever brains there are in the family, I've got them. Ask George—he'll tell you as much himself."

"I don't have to ask him," Johnny said. "You not only seem to have the brains, you've also got..."

She looked down at her slender, perfectly shaped legs. There was a coy smile around her mouth.

"I know what I've got," she said. "I still want to know about the 'business' deal."

The idea of telling her never crossed his mind. That she was smart, he was well aware. Probably a lot smarter than her husband. But she was also dynamite. He knew that he would have to tell her something, however.

"All right," he said. "Here it is. George is around the track a lot. A cashier gets to hear things. Several of us—the men you saw in the other room, have a betting syndicate. We want to have George get us certain information from some of the jocks. In case we win, we cut him in on the take. It's as simple as that."

She looked at him without change of expression.

He's cagey, she thought, very cagey. That's good. Maybe, just maybe, the stickup plan might really work.

Johnny himself was wondering if she'd go for the story. If she did, then he could worry. He knew that she was smart; and a smart girl would know that George would have no information to peddle. He waited, anxiously, for her next words.

"You guys must be nuts," she said then. "My God, don't you think that if old Georgie knew anything, had any real information, we'd be using it ourselves?"

"Maybe your husband is smarter than you think," Johnny said.

Sherry Peatty laughed.

"The only smart thing George ever did was talk me into marrying him."

"That was smart?"

She pouted.

"What do you think?"

"I think he was lucky."

She walked over to him. Leaning down, she lightly brushed his lips with her own.

"You're nice," she said. "When am I going to see you?"

He thought for a minute. He wanted to see her again. He wanted to be dead sure she didn't know anything.

"Well," he said, "that's up to you. Right now, I'm staying in this dump. And for certain reasons, I've got to stay around the place for the next few days. If you want to show up the first of the week, say Monday around two o'clock, we might have a little party. Can't promise you much except Scotch and..."

"And what..."

"You name it," Johnny said.

She smiled at him.

"I'll be here, Monday at two. And we can name it together. Only remember one thing, no more rough stuff. I don't take that from anyone."

He nodded and stood up.

"It's a deal," he said. "By the way, how does George feel about you having dates?"

"George won't know."

"Oke."

He went into the other room with her and waited while she made up her face.

"I'd take you home," he began, "but..."

"I know," she said. "But you better not. You're right."

She reached for the doorknob and he started toward her, but she put up one hand.

"Monday," she said.

She closed the door softly behind herself.

Johnny went back into the bedroom and retrieved the bottle. It was almost empty. He poured himself a small drink, went into the kitchen and mixed it with water.

He was lifting the glass when the phone rang.

* * * * *

It was a blue Dodge sedan, less than a year old, and Mike drove after Randy showed him about the automatic shift. "Go up to Central Park and we'll circle around slowly," Randy said. "And for Christ sake drive careful; I still owe twelve hundred on this buggy."

Big Mike nodded, climbed behind the wheel. Randy got in back with George Peatty. He pulled a pack of cigarettes from his pocket but didn't offer one to the other man. He was silent as the car weaved through traffic, and headed up Fifth Avenue.

Peatty couldn't hold it any more.

"Look," he said, "he won't hurt her, will he? She doesn't know anything, couldn't cause any trouble. She..."

"He won't hurt her," Randy said. "No, he won't hurt her. But I might hurt you."

"I tell you I didn't say a word," George said. He'd begun to lose his fear and his voice was petulant. "My god, this thing means as much to me as..."

"If it means something to you, then it's about time you smartened up a little."

"You're not married," George said. "You don't understand about wives. She was just suspicious because I was going out."

"O.K.," Randy said. "We'll leave it at that for the time being. Just shut up now."

They drove slowly around the park for the better part of an hour and then Randy asked George for his address. Minutes later Mike found a parking spot in front of the house. All three men entered. They sat in George Peatty's living room and he asked if anyone wanted a drink. Mike and Randy both declined.

"Get me a phone book," Randy said.

George went over to a sideboard and got the Manhattan directory. Randy thumbed the pages. He stood up, holding the book opened, and went to the phone. He dialed Unger's number.

Johnny answered on the second ring.

"Randy," the cop said in a soft voice. "What's the score?"

"Where are you?"

"We got Peatty with us, at his place."

"Good," Johnny said. "I think everything is O.K. You can leave him now. The girl's on her way home. You and Mike get back here. We'll decide what to do then."

"And Peatty?"

"Just tell him to keep his mouth shut. Tell him to call this number tomorrow night, after he gets off work. When you and Mike get back we can decide things."

Randy grunted and hung up the receiver.

"You're to call Unger's place tomorrow as soon as you get off work," he said, turning to Peatty. "Come on, Mike."

Mike stood up. He looked over at George.

"How about..."

"Sorry we got rough," Randy cut in. "But it certainly didn't look right, your wife showing up. Anyway, Johnny says everything is O.K. Just be sure to keep your lips buttoned. And control that wife of yours. Call Johnny tomorrow."

He walked out of the room, followed by Big Mike.

They arrived back at the Thirty-first Street apartment house as Unger was ringing his own downstairs doorbell. It was just after eleven o'clock.

The dark, saturnine man sitting behind the wheel of the Cadillac convertible reached forward and switched off the car radio as the Dodge pulled up across the street. He turned to his companion and spoke softly.

"Those are the two that left with her husband," he said. A shake of his head indicated Mike and Randy as they reached the outside door of the apartment.

"Wonder what happened to the other guy?"

Val Cannon laughed softly.

"Peatty? Hell, they probably took him home and put him to bed."

"Maybe we should of stopped the girl when she came out?"

"No. Someone could have been watching from upstairs. I'll see her tomorrow. And I hope she found out something. Incidentally, I got news for you."

The short, heavy-set man at his side looked up at him with sudden curiosity.

"Yeah?"

"Yeah. The tall guy with the broad shoulders is a cop. Works a patrol car in the upper midtown district. Name's Kennan."

His companion whistled softly.

"A cop," he said. "Now I wonder..."

"I wonder too."

Cannon pushed the starter button and a moment later the Caddie pulled silently and smoothly away from the curb. He was nodding his head and his words were almost inaudible.

"It could be," he said. "It certainly could be."

* * * * *

Marvin Unger's observant eyes quickly darted around the apartment when he entered. He walked through the living room, into the bedroom, took off his hat and put it on the dresser. Unconsciously he straightened the chair which had fallen into one corner. He noticed at once the mussed up bed and his thin lips twisted in an unpleasant grin.

The others were seated around the table when he came out.

"What did you do, have a wrestling match?" he asked, his voice nasty.

Johnny ignored the remark. He continued talking to the others.

"And so," he said, "I really don't think she heard anything. I can't be sure, but I don't think so. It was probably like both she and George said. He got careless and she found the address. Being a dame, she was curious and she followed him here."

Randy grunted something under his breath. Big Mike nodded.

"So what do we do now?" Unger asked.

"We go right ahead," Johnny said. "In the first place, George knows too much to drop him out at this stage. Also, we need him. Without him, it's too risky. He's got the plans for the inside work; he knows the details."

"We couldn't drop him anyway," Randy said. "Not with what he knows."

"There's no need to drop him. He's a weak sister, but that part doesn't matter. All of his work will be done before we pull the job."

"Yeah, but how about afterward?" Randy asked. "How about when the law starts questioning him? And you can bet your bottom buck he'll be questioned. Everybody will. Everyone who works around the track or who could possibly know anything. You can be sure of that."

Johnny nodded, thoughtfully.

"I know," he said. "On the other hand, I had that part figured all along. Yes, he'll be questioned, and he is a weak sister. But I don't think he'll crack. After all, he won't get too much pressure. And another thing, I think his main weakness involves that wife of his. Outside of where she's concerned, George is all right."

"A woman like that..." Unger began.

"A woman like that," Johnny said, "likes dough. Likes it more than anything else in the world. She may have her own ideas, after everything is over and done with. In fact she's sure to figure the pitch. But remember one thing. George is in this for only one reason. To get money for her. He knows it and she will know it, once he's got his cut. And she's tough. A hell of a lot tougher than he is. You can bet that she'll protect his end of it."

Unger stopped pacing and sat down.

"Well, I don't know," he said. "I can't say I like it. That kind of people. They don't seem very reliable. No stamina. Hardly the type to be in on a thing like this."

Johnny turned to him, frowning.

"Jesus," he said, "be sensible. That's why this thing is going to work. We don't want a lot of hoodlums in on it. Take yourself; you're not tough certainly. But I think you're right for this. It's what I've been telling you guys from the beginning. We aren't a bunch of dumb stick-up artists. We aren't tough guys. We're supposed to have brains. Well, George Peatty may not burn the world up, but he's bright enough and he's reliable enough, too. The thing is not to give him something to do which is over his head."

He stopped for a minute and took a deep breath.

"That's the beauty of this deal. George is doing the planning on the caper, the blueprint work. For that he's good. Mike fits in the same way and will also help a little at the time we pull the job. Randy and I are the ones who really run the chances. Take the risks on any violence. And we're equipped to do what we have to do."

Randy Kennan looked up at him and nodded slowly.

"Right," he said.

Unger sat down then. He looked satisfied.

"All right," he said, "let's get down to business."

Johnny took a notebook from his pocket, opened it and began reading.

It wasn't that she was afraid to go home. Afraid of what George would say. No, nothing he might say or do could possibly worry her. The fact that she might have been responsible for getting him beaten up, didn't bother her in the slightest. But one thing did worry her. Would the gang still play along with him? Thinking about it, she realized that they couldn't very well afford to get rid of him at this late date.

But then there was the other factor. How about George himself?

She knew him like a book; knew his strengths and knew his weaknesses. Would George himself be scared and back off? It was more than possible. Sherry was sorry that she had listened to Val Cannon. Not sorry that she'd told him about the plot, but sorry that she'd gone up to the apartment. It had been foolish. She had, she realized, put the entire operation in jeopardy. She thought of Johnny—Johnny Clay.

He interested her. He was a man like Val, a man who appealed to her. She liked men with strength and he had been strong. Thinking of him, she began to feel optimistic about the robbery. He would be the boy to handle it all right.

She felt hungry and so she stopped off at a Broadway chophouse and took a small table. The place wasn't crowded and she ordered a Manhattan and a club steak. She wanted to think over how she'd handle George when she got home. It would be tricky. But she didn't worry. There was one way she could always handle him; one thing he always wanted and which it was within her power to either give or withhold.

She drank her Manhattan and then, while she waited for the food to come, searched in her bag and found a dime. She got up and went to a phone booth at the rear.

George answered immediately and she breathed a little easier. She was glad he was home.

"You alone, George?" she asked, before he had a chance to say more than hello.

He started at once to ask where she was and if she was all right.

She cut in on him.

"Listen," she said, "just stay there until I get home. I'm all right; I'm fine. Don't worry about me. But just stay there. I'll be along in less than an hour."

He started again to ask questions, but she hung up.

Waiting would give him a chance to cool off.

By the time she had finished eating she was feeling fine. She ordered a B and B and lingered over it. Then she called for a check, paid it and went out. She found a cruising cab within a block and climbed in, giving the driver her address.

George was sitting in his undershirt in the living room, with all the lights on, staring at the door, when she entered. There was a dark purple bruise under one eye and he looked sick. His hands began to shake as he got up.

"Sherry," he said. "Oh Jesus, Sherry! Did they hurt you? Did they..."

"Relax, George," she said, closing the door behind her and tossing her bag on the table. "Relax and get me a drink."

"Sherry," he said, walking toward her. "My God, Sherry, you could have got us both killed."

"I said get me a drink, George. And get yourself one, too. You look like you need it. And don't start in with recriminations. We have important things to talk about."

He hunched his narrow shoulders and turned toward the kitchen. He was mumbling as he went.

She went over to the upholstered chair in which he had been sitting and slumped down in it and sighed. It would be just like handling a child. Get him to do what she wanted him to do, and then give him his reward.

George returned with the drinks and handed her one. He started to sit on the edge of her chair, but she told him to go over to the couch.

"What ever made you come up there, Sherry?" he asked. "How did you know where..."

"I found the address in your pocket, George."

He blushed.

"Jesus, Sherry..."

"Never mind the post-mortems," she said, quickly. "We've got more important things to talk about. Those were the men, weren't they? The ones you're in with on the stick-up deal?"

He nodded.

"Yes. Those were the men. But Sherry, the hell with it. I don't want it. It's too dangerous. I don't know what I could have been thinking about. It isn't only the robbery itself. God knows that's risky enough. But these men, they aren't fooling around. They could have killed you as easily as not. They could have killed us both."

"Don't be a damned fool," Sherry said. "They had no reason to kill me. And they can't afford to kill you. They need you, don't they?"

"What did Johnny say to you?" George asked. "What did he do?"

"He wanted to know what I was doing outside the door. I just told him that I followed you to the place. I told him I didn't hear a thing, and in fact, I didn't."

"And he believed you?"

"Of course he believed me."

"You don't realize it, Sherry, but although Johnny is a nice enough guy, he's plenty tough. Why, he just got done doing four years in Sing Sing."

"He did?" She laughed lightly. "He isn't tough, George."

"Did he try to..."

"I can handle guys like him with my hands tied behind me," she said. "Duck soup."

He stared at her, worry in his eyes.

She got up, went over to the couch. She didn't want to be questioned any more and so she sat down, half on his lap, and carelessly touched the bruise over his eye.

"Listen, George," she said. "I want you to go through with it. There's nothing to worry about. It's all over now. I'll admit I was foolish to go there, but in a way it serves you right. You've got to take me into your confidence, let me know what you are planning to do. Somebody's got to look out for you."

She snuggled deeper into his lap and caressed his face with her hands.

"But Sherry," he said, "I'm going to quit; give it up."

She stiffened, started to say something, then as quickly relaxed. She stood up and pulled gently at his arm.

"Right now," she said, "you're coming to bed. You still have to work tomorrow and you must be dead on your feet."

Undressing in the bathroom, with the door partly closed, she smiled wryly. She could hear George in the other room, carefully removing his own clothes. He'd be folding his trousers, putting them over the back of a chair; hanging up the rest of his garments neatly. He'd be hurrying, but still neat and orderly.

George's pattern of behavior, his mentality, never varied. After two years of marriage, she knew him like a book. He was ABC. She knew. They'd gone through the same act a hundred times.

His stubbornness was one of the basic contradictions to his character. She knew that once he had made up his mind to something, it was almost impossible to move him. Almost, but not quite. She knew just what would happen. He was determined to give up, quit the whole thing. He was equally determined not to tell her any more details of the plan.

She shrugged, looked at herself in the mirror, standing there completely naked and lovely. She cocked her head, saucily; smiled at her own image.

It would be like taking candy from a child.

He was in bed when she came in; the lights were off except for the small table lamp which threw a shaded glow at one side of the double bed. Half consciously, she noticed that George hadn't opened the window for the night. Once more she smiled, this time inwardly.

George was about as subtle as a fractured pelvis.

She hesitated for just a moment, knew that he was watching

her covertly. Then she lifted back the sheet and crawled in next to him. She knew better than to begin questioning him.

It was the same as it always was when she wanted something. She'd tantalize him, then draw away. Carefully lead him on, but every time at the last moment, deny him. It had to end up as it always did. George finally asserted himself.

Later, he was completely convinced that he had raped her.

It always ended up the same way. His exhaustion, his subtle conviction that he had found his manhood, his sentimentality and then his fumbling apologies and his pleas for forgiveness.

She handled the scene with all the artistry and finesse of a first-class dramatic actress—which, in a sense, she was.

An hour after they had retired, George agreed to stick with the others and see the thing through. He'd do it for her, Sherry, to whom he owed so much and from whom he had taken so much.

But that was as far as he would go. He refused to tell her any more about it. Refused to discuss details, or when it was to happen, or how it was to happen.

She didn't push him. She knew that sooner or later, they'd repeat the matrimonial travesty and she'd find out what she had to find out.

He had turned over on his side and was snoring lightly as she got out of bed and crossed the room and lifted the window several inches.

Much later, lying on her back and smoking a cigarette in the dark, she thought of Val Cannon. She felt an almost unbearable desire for him.

The strange part of it was, after she had butted the cigarette in the ash tray at the side of the bed and was finally lost in that strange semiconsciousness between wakefulness and sleep, the image of Val Cannon and that of Johnny Clay kept blending together and becoming one.

She finally fell completely asleep and the expression on her tired, pretty face was one of discontent.

✳CHAPTER V✣

Nikki stretched a lean, corded arm up over his head and felt around blindly until his fingers found the square of chalk hanging from the string. Brown eyes still studying the table, he worked on the end of the cue tip.

He smiled, without mirth but at the same time with no viciousness, and didn't look at his opponent as he spoke.

"You're a sucker," he said. "A real first-class sucker. So I'll give you a buck even on the six in the side pocket—and I'll play it off the ten ball."

"You got it!"

The small, wizened man with the face of a half starved coyote, perched on the high stool at the side of the table, turned to his fat companion.

"Can't be done," he said. "Willy Hoppe himself couldn't do it."

Nikki heard him.

"For you," he said over his shoulder, "I'll give you ten bucks to five it can be done. Ten to five I do it."

"Take him," the fat man said.

"Take him hell," said the other. "I just said it can't be done—I didn't say Nikki couldn't do it."

Nikki finished chalking his cue, released the chalk and walked around to the side of the pool table. He leaned over, carefully studied the lay. And then he leveled the stick and sighting along its straight surface, made his shot. The cue ball rolled straight and true and barely grazed the ten, swerved at an oblique angle to strike the six. The green ball rolled with infinite slowness and plunked into the side pocket.

Johnny Clay walked into the billiard parlor as Nikki raised the cue from his follow-up position, his face expressionless.

"That boy's got an eye like a bomb sight," the fat man said.

Johnny didn't approach the table, but stopped at the bar and ordered a beer. Nikki saw him at once.

Johnny waited until Nikki had racked his cue, collected his bets and reached for his coat. Then he downed the beer and went back outside. Nikki followed him out—caught up with him a few yards from the entrance. He fell in step and spoke out of the side of his mouth, his lips barely moving.

"Jesus, Johnny," he said, "when did they spring you?"

"Tell you later," Johnny said, looking straight ahead. "Grab off a cab."

Five minutes later they were in the back of a yellow taxi, the window closed between themselves and the driver, who had been given the address of a midtown hotel.

Johnny waited until they were in Nikki's room before he spoke.

"You got the letter?"

Nikki stripped off his jacket, tossed it on the bed and shrugged as it slipped off to the floor. He didn't move the gray felt hat, cocked over one eye. He leaned against the dresser.

"I got it, Johnny," he said. "And you could a knocked me over with a damp feather when the five bills rolled out. What's the pitch? I thought you were still in the house."

"I've been out for a little while," Johnny said. "Probation. I was still in when the letter was sent you."

Nikki nodded.

"I figured when there was no signature. But I knew where it came from."

He paused a moment, watching Johnny closely. "You're looking good, boy."

"Feeling good," Johnny said. "What's with you?"

"Taking it easy," Nikki said. "Three up and one to go. So I'm taking it easy. Got a policy job nights. But about the five bills, Johnny. I suppose..." his voice drifted off.

"Right," Johnny said. "I want it. The chopper."

"That's what I figured, Johnny, when the dough dropped out. I got it all ready for you."

He pulled a cheap, imitation leather suitcase from under the bed, inserted a key from a ring he carried in his side pocket. A moment later he tossed open the top and took out a long, heavy bundle wrapped up in a Turkish towel. He carried it over to the bed and unwrapped it. It was a broken down Thompson sub-machine gun.

"Pretty baby," he said.

He began to assemble it.

"These things are hard to come by today," he went on, working steadily, his lean strong fingers finding the parts automatically. "Very hard to come by. Know anything about them?"

Johnny half shook his head.

"I only know what they're for," he said.

Nikki nodded.

"Well, they're really simple enough. This is an old-timer; probably left over from prohibition days. But it speaks with just as much authority as the new ones. It's simple; I'll show you how it's done." He reached for a clip.

"This thing holds exactly twenty-five shots. You want to re-member that. Twenty-five. Most jobs shouldn't take that much. I'm giving you three extra clips, just in case. But remember one thing. The chances are pretty much against your having time to reload, in case baby has to talk."

Johnny nodded, watching him intently.

"If you do use her, remember to touch her just lightly, very lightly. One burst will release five or six shots a lot faster than you can count them. Don't throw them away or you're likely to end up holding a piece of dead iron in your mittens while someone is taking potshots at you.

"Also, watch the accuracy. Don't stand too far away; don't try to use this as a sporting rifle. It's designed for close quarters. And don't shoot it at all unless you're ready to kill. You hit 'em once and the chances are you hit 'em half a dozen times. Too much lead to be anything but fatal."

Johnny reached over and touched the barrel.

"Looks plenty lethal," he said.

"It is. That's the beauty of it. They only have to see it and they behave right proper. Even the heroes don't give a typewriter an argument."

For the next few minutes he explained the operation of the gun, showing Johnny the safety catch and the various mechanisms. He then went over breaking the gun down and putting it together. Finally he rewrapped it and put it back in the suitcase. He closed the bag and took the small key off the ring and handed it to Johnny.

"I'll throw in the keister for free," he said.

Johnny reached for the bag, put it between his feet and then sat down on the edge of the bed.

"One more little thing," he said.

Nikki looked up at him sharply.

"Yes?"

"You say you're working policy. Right? Can't be too much in it."

"There isn't," Nikki said. "But also there isn't much trouble in it, either."

"That's right," Johnny said. "On the other hand, there isn't much trouble in five thousand dollars."

For a second Nikki just stared at him. Then he walked slowly over to the exposed sink in the corner of the room, took a half pint flask from the shelf above it, which also held his razor and his toothbrush. He took his time and poured a stiff shot into a plastic toothbrush glass and handed it to Johnny. He lifted the flask to his own lips, wordlessly, his eyes on the other man.

Johnny nodded, grinned, drank.

Nikki took the bottle neck from his mouth, coughed and tossed the empty flask into a half filled trash basket; walked across the room and sat in a broken leather chair. He leaned forward, facing Johnny, his slender, long fingered hands clasping each other between his bony knees.

"Who do I have to kill?"

Johnny looked him straight in the eye, unsmiling.

"A horse," he said.

Nikki blinked.

"A horse? You mean a horse's..."

"A horse," Johnny said. "A four-legged horse."

For a minute Nikki just stared at him. Then he slouched to his feet.

"All right," he said, "so you're on the junk. Too bad."

Johnny didn't get up.

"I'm giving it to you straight, boy," he said. "I want you to shoot a horse."

"And for that I get five thousand dollars?"

"For that and..."

"Yeah, and. I figured there had to be a gimmick."

"Not a bad gimmick," Johnny said. "The 'and' isn't as tough as it sounds. You shoot a horse and, if by any chance you get picked up, you don't crack. Under no conditions do you crack. That's all."

"You mean," Nikki said, still looking baffled, "all I got to do is bump a horse."

"It's a special horse, Nikki."

"So-o-o?"

"I better give it to you," Johnny said. "For certain reasons, including your own protection in case anything happens, I'm not going to tell you the whole story. Just your part.

"Next Saturday, a week from today, the Canarsie Stakes are being run. Seventh race—the big race of the year."

He was watching the other man closely as he talked and he saw his mouth turn down in a twisted smile as he slowly nodded his head.

"There's a horse in that race—Black Lightning—one of the best three-year-olds to come along in the last ten years. A big money winner. He won't pay even money. Just about half of that crowd out there is going to be down on him. Well, there's a parking lot less than three hundred feet from the northwest end of the track. From a car sitting in the southeast corner of that lot, you get a perfect view of the horses as they come around the far corner and start into the stretch. A man, sitting in a car parked in that spot, using a high caliber rifle with a telescopic sight, should be able to bring down any given horse with a single shot. A man with your eye wouldn't hardly need the telescopic sight."

For a minute Nikki looked at him, completely aghast.

"Jesus Christ!" he said at last. "Je-zuz Key-rist!"

"Right," said Johnny.

"Why, that horse is worth a quarter of a million bucks," Nikki said. "The crowd would go completely nuts. Nuts, I tell you."

"So what," Johnny said. "Let 'em go nuts. You could do it—easy. And you shouldn't have too much trouble getting away in the confusion. Black Lightning will, without doubt, be leading into the stretch. He runs that way, takes an early lead and keeps it. So he goes down, a half dozen others are going to pile up on him. There'll be plenty of damn excitement."

"For the first time you're making sense," Nikki said. "There sure as hell would be."

"That's the point," Johnny said. "So in the excitement, you make your getaway. For five grand you can afford to leave the rifle behind. And another thing, suppose by accident you do get picked up. What have you done? Well, you shot a horse. It's not first degree murder. In fact it isn't even murder. I don't know what the hell it would be, but the chances are the best they could get you for would be inciting to a riot or shooting out-of-season or something."

Nikki sat slowly shaking his head.

"The way you say it, kid," he said, "you make it sound simple as hell. But Jesus Christ, knocking over the favorite in the Canarsie Stakes! Brother."

"Five thousand," Johnny said. "Five thousand bucks for rubbing out a horse."

Nikki looked up and all at once Johnny knew he was in.

"How do I get it?"

"Twenty-five hundred on Monday afternoon. The rest one day after the race."

Nikki nodded.

"And what's your angle, Johnny? Why are you willing to pay five grand to knock off Black Lightning? Hell, the horse gets killed and they probably call off the race."

"Maybe," Johnny said. "But what my angle is, is my business. And, Nikki, that's why I'm paying five grand, so nobody has to know my business."

Nikki nodded.

"Sure," he said.

They talked over the details for another half hour and finally Johnny stood up to leave. He reached down for the suitcase.

"So I'll see you Monday, Nikki," he said. "I'll have the map with me."

* * * * *

Maurice Cohen's mother answered the doorbell. A short, dumpy near-sighted woman with gray streaks showing through the henna of her carefully marcelled hair, she held a dressing gown across her huge breasts with one tightly clutched hand. She was careful to keep the door itself on the safety chain. These days you could never tell who was wandering around the Bronx, as likely as not ready to rob and murder you right in your own living room.

"Mister Cohen?" Johnny said.

"Mister Cohen ain't home. He's at work. Where he should be in the afternoon. At work."

She started to close the door.

"Mister Maurice Cohen," Johnny said.

"Ah, Maurice," she said. "He's in bed. Who shall I say?"

"Mr. Clay," Johnny said.

She closed the door without another word. Johnny waited in

the halfway of the apartment house, leaning against the wall and lighting a cigarette. Five minutes later the door again opened. A tall, deceptively slender, dark boy who didn't look more than twenty-one or -two, slid out. He wore a sports shirt, a thin, well-creased suit and tan, openwork shoes. He was smoking a cigar.

His eyes lit up with surprise and recognition when he spotted Johnny.

"Johnny," he said. "Well for God's sake, Johnny."

His mother was calling something after him as they entered the self-service elevator. He didn't pay any attention as he pushed the button for the main floor.

They went to a bar and grill a half a block away and took a booth at the back. The place was empty except for an aproned bartender and a faded looking blonde who sat at the end of the bar and stared at an empty highball glass.

The bartender brought them two bottles of beer and two glasses and Johnny got up and went to the juke box. He dropped a quarter in the slot and pushed five buttons at random. The blonde looked up at him, vacant-eyed, as he returned to the booth.

"I got your letter," Maurice said, above the noise of the machine.

Johnny nodded.

"What you been doing with yourself since you been out, Maurice?"

The slender, almost effeminate youth looked at him and smiled without humor.

"You wrote you had something to tell me, not ask me," he said.

Johnny laughed.

"Right," he said. "I was just making talk. I want to tell you how you can make $2500."

"That's different," Maurice said. "All right, I been doing nothing. I'm supposed to be working with my old man; as you know, I'm on pro. But I can't take the hours. So I stay in bed most of the day and then I just wander around nights. I'm watching the corners until I get clear again."

He watched Johnny closely as he talked and went on after stopping to take a sip of beer.

"I'm thinking about things," he said. "No more rough stuff for me. One rap was one too many. Twenty-five hundred sounds very interesting according to what I got to do to get it. No guns, though."

"No guns," Johnny said. "Maurice, you used to play football in high school—that right?"

"Right," Maurice said. "I was the lightest tackle old Washington Heights ever had. Good, if I say so myself. But what the hell—you ain't running a football team, are you, Johnny."

"No, I am not. But I'm ready to pay you—or some other guy—twenty-five C's to run a little interference."

"With cops?"

"With cops—private cops."

"Start all over," Maurice said, "and tell me about it. Tell me the whole story. For that kind of dough, it must be some interference. But remember one thing, I might go for the deal but as I say, no guns. Also, I want nobody taking potshots at me, either. How tough are those private cops going to be?"

"Here's the story," Johnny said. "I'm only going to give you your end of it. That's why I'm willing to pay big dough—for what you do and for what you don't have to know.

"I want you out at the track during the running of the Canarsie Stakes a week from today. In the clubhouse, near the bar at the center door. I'll give you the details later. It so happens I know that there's going to be quite a little riot going on—say just about at the end of the big race. You are going to be at the bar and during the first part of that little riot, you are to do nothing—nothing except keep your eye on the door leading into the main business office, about thirty feet from the bar where you will be standing. You are a casual bystander.

"Along about the middle of that little riot, that door is going to open and I'm coming out of it. Fast. I'm slamming the door behind me and I want to melt away into the crowd."

"What crowd?" Maurice said. "I thought you said this will be during the big race. The crowd will all be out in the stands."

"There will also be a lot of people between the bar and that door," Johnny said. "I told you there will be a small riot going on. Just take my word for it. Anyway, I'm coming out of that door. There is every chance no one will follow me, at least for about fifteen seconds. But there is also a chance that someone might. You are to stop them. Anyway you can—slug them, give them a bum steer as to the direction I have taken, get in their way—do anything you have to. But be there and be damn sure that I have a chance to mix in with the crowd."

"What will you be carrying?" Maurice asked, his eyes wise.

Johnny watched the other man closely for a second, and then continued. "If I carry anything, I will drop it," he said, "as soon as I slam that door behind me. It will be a chopper. That's when you go into action. There is a good chance no one but you will see me. The minute I drop that gun, you yell. Something like, 'Look out—he's got a gun!' Bring attention to it, once I'm clear of it. That door is going to fly open and they'll be after me within seconds. You got to get them going in the wrong direction. If necessary, you got to stop them. Get in their way, do anything, but stop them. I've got to have a chance to get out of the clubhouse."

Maurice looked at him shrewdly. "You'll never get away with it," he said.

"Get away with what?"

"Why, Goddamn it, you know..."

"Twenty-five hundred, Maurice," Johnny said, "is so you won't know. I just told you, I'm dropping that gun at the door and I'm leaving clean. I'm not getting away with anything."

Maurice again shrugged.

"You got to tell me more," he said.

"No, I don't, kid. I'm offering you a lotta dough so I don't have to tell you."

"Yeah, an' suppose I get picked up?"

"So what? What have you done? Nothing. You are at the track, a riot starts. You are as excited as everyone else. You see a guy run. That's no crime. Maybe you get in the way.

"There's one more thing. I come out of that door with a handkerchief over my face. I take it off the sec I slam the door behind me. I also have on a yellow checked sports jacket and a soft gray hat, pulled over my eyes. Well, when I drop that handkerchief, and I hope it's before anyone but you see me, I also start stripping out of that coat and get rid of the hat. I'll have another hat with me, and I'll have a sports shirt on under the jacket. What they'll look like, you won't have to know. But if and when anyone starts asking questions, just be sure about your description of me. That is, be sure it's all wrong."

"You figure a Pinkerton will be coming out of that door after you?"

"I know one will—unless the chopper is hot when I drop it and I don't want it that way. You're to see that the detective gets mixed up before he has a chance to get anywhere. Trip him, fall into him, slug him if you have to. You can always say you didn't realize he was a cop and that he jostled you. You'll know he's a private cop all right, but there is no reason you should.

"They'll question you if they pick you up. On the other hand, in the confusion, you may get clear. Either way, you are just a patron at the track, an innocent bystander and a guy runs into you and you slug him."

"It could cost me my parole," Maurice said. "Just being at the track could..."

"That's another reason you get the twenty-five bills," Johnny said. "You got to take that chance."

"And if I get picked up and they find out about my record, it can cost me one hell of a beating."

"What kind of dough did you get the last time you were in the ring in that Golden Gloves fight?" Johnny asked softly. "The one where you got the broken ribs and the injury to your optic nerve."

Maurice smiled thinly.

"I gotta bronze medal," he said.

"All right, so they question you. You don't know nothing. They beat hell out of you. You still don't know nothing. Twenty-five hundred is a lot better than a bronze medal."

"It is. But there is also the business about breaking parole."

"That's right," Johnny said. "And that's why you get real money. For taking that chance."

"I don't quite understand this whole thing," Maurice said. "Hell, Johnny, for what you want me to do, any hoodlum would handle for a hundred bucks."

Johnny picked up the two empty bottles and went over to the bar. He got a couple of refills and came back to the table, dropping another coin into the juke box as he passed.

He sat down, poured the glasses full, leaving an inch of foam.

"Not any hoodlum, kid," he said. "I don't want a hoodlum; I want a smart guy. A guy smart enough not only to do the job and that I can depend upon, but a guy smart enough to know that he is being well paid to take a chance and that if things don't turn out just right, he won't squawk. That he'll remember that he is being well paid."

Maurice nodded.

"I don't suppose," he said, "that you feel like cutting me in on a piece of the job itself—and let's say we skip the twenty-five cash?"

"Can't," Johnny said. "It isn't mine to cut up."

Maurice slowly nodded.

"I'm your boy," he said. "When...?"

"Monday afternoon, here. I'll have a grand at that time and full instructions." He stood up.

"I'll hang around here for a few minutes," Maurice said. He smiled, held out his hand.

Johnny shook hands with him.

"Tell your mother," he said, "that that burglary chain would give with one good shove. I'll be seeing you."

"I'll buy her a new one—after the race," Maurice said.

A thin, harassed-looking man in a sweat shirt four sizes too big for him told Johnny at Stillman's that he hadn't seen Tex around in a couple of weeks or more.

"He won't train," the man said, "so goddamn it, I hope he don't ever come back. He could be a good boy if he'd only train."

Johnny thanked him and went downstairs and got into a cab. He didn't want to be walking around the midtown district in broad daylight. He gave the driver the address of a third-rate hotel down on West Broadway.

Tex had left the day before, and from the way the day clerk acted, he left without paying his bill.

Another cab dropped Johnny at Third Avenue and East Eighth Street and he started downtown, systematically making the stops at every bar. He found Tex at his fourth stop, leaning against a juke box, his squinty blue eyes misty and his head slowly weaving back and forth in time with the music. Tex didn't see him when he entered and went to the bar. Johnny ordered a Scotch with water on the side.

"That son of a bitch plays Danny Boy just one more time and I throw him out," the bartender said, sliding the glass across the bar. "Jesus!"

Johnny swallowed his drink, washed it down. He left a quarter for the bartender and went to the juke box. He put a quarter in the machine and carefully selected Danny Boy wouldn't be in, that he was home sick and expected to be all right the following day.

Then he went back to the bar and ordered another drink. There was no point in kidding himself. Sherry was a tramp. She was a tramp and she was a liar.

She'd come home last night with lipstick smeared all over her face. Her breath reeked of liquor. She had been with no sick girl friend. She'd been with some man, lapping up whiskey and God only knows what else.

George ordered another drink.

He wasn't, at the moment, curious as to who the man might be. It was enough to finally admit that Sherry was running around with other men. But the fact, once he was willing to accept the truth, was irrefutable.

At once George began to feel sorry for Sherry and to blame himself. If she was running with other men, it could only mean that he had failed her. George felt a tear come to the corner of his eye and he was about to beckon the waiter to refill his glass. It was then that he caught sight of his face in the mirror behind the stacks of pyramided bottles. In a split second he sobered up completely.

What kind of god damned idiot was he? Good God, here it was the most important week in his life and he was standing at a public bar getting drunk. He should have been at the track. The last thing in the world he should have done was to have failed to follow the usual routine of his days.

Quickly he turned from the bar, not bothering to pick up his change. Well, it was too late now to make the track, but at least he would go out and get some food into his stomach and some hot coffee. Then he would go to a movie and take it easy. He fully realized how essential it was that he be completely sober before evening.

Tonight was the big meeting. And he, George, wanted to get there a little before the meeting. He wanted to talk to Johnny alone for a minute or two before the others arrived. He wanted to assure Johnny that they would have nothing to worry about as far as he, George, was concerned.

* * * * *

"Pinched?"

"Right," Johnny said. "For certain reasons of my own, you gotta be pinched. And I want you to make it good. If it takes two cops to get you out of the place, so much the better."

"I can take half a dozen," Tex said. "Private cops? Hell, Johnny, I can make it take a full dozen. I..."

"Two will be fine," Johnny said and smiled. "I don't want you hurt either."

"Do I ask any questions, Johnny?"

"No. Not now or later. Here's what you have to know and all I want you to know."

He talked then for the better part of a half hour, going over much of the same material he had discussed with the two other men he had seen that day. Tex, however, differed from the others in that he showed not the slightest curiosity. It was good enough for him the way Johnny put it. He was being given a job to do, he was getting paid for it, he would do it.

"There's just the one thing," Johnny said. "Timing. You got to time it exactly right. On the button."

"I got no watch," Tex said.

"You won't need one," Johnny told him. "There's a big clock right over the center of the bar. One thing you got to be sure of; keep the fight going long enough so the cops show. And then get them to rush you out of there as quick as you can."

"Hell," Tex said, "I can keep 'em busy for a half hour, you want I should."

"I don't," Johnny told him. "Getting out, that is, getting the cops out, is the whole deal. You have to time it perfectly."

The big man nodded.

"An' for that I get twenty-five hun'ert?"

"For that Tex, and for taking the rap which you will be sure to get. Probably about ninety days. Also there will be a lotta questions thrown at you. Why you did it, who you know and all the rest of it."

"I did it because the goddamn bartender tried to cheat me. I don't know nobody. Right?"

"You got it perfect," Johnny said. "I wish there were more like you." He hesitated a second, then went on. "I can get you about half the dough by Monday, the rest after it's all over."

"Your word's good with me, laddie," Tex said. "You can make it all after, if you want to. In fac', you can wait till I get out of the clink. That's if they got enough guys there to get me that far."

"They got enough, Tex," Johnny said. "No, we'll do it my way;

say a grand on Monday and fifteen as soon as I can get it to you after Saturday."

Tex nodded, satisfied.

"I hate to ask it," he said, "but I could use something like a twenty in cash right now."

Johnny reached into his pocket and peeled a twenty from the money Marvin Unger had left with him that morning.

"Monday Tex," he said. "Here. And for Christ sake, keep out of trouble until after this is over."

"Hell, Johnny," the big man said, "you don' have to worry 'bout me. I'm your boy."

Johnny stood up and patted him on the back, then left, word-lessly.

The suitcase was in the corner of the double parcel locker on the upper level at Grand Central when Johnny stopped back for it. Carrying it made him nervous, but there was nothing much he could do about that. He took the uptown IRT subway to Ninety-sixth Street and got off. Walking uptown to a Hundred and Third, he turned toward the East River. He found the place he was looking for just West of Second Avenue. It was an old law tenement, with its face lifted. He rang the bell on the ground floor and a moment later a sallow, hard-faced man stood outside the iron grill.

* * * * *

"Looking for Joe Piano," Johnny said.

"Who's looking for Joe?"

"Patsy sent me."

"Patsy who?"

"Patsy Genelli."

The man made no move to open the door.

"And where did you see Patsy?" he asked.

"Ossining. We roomed together. I'm..."

"Don't tell me who you are," the man said.

He twisted the knob and the lock clicked and he opened the gate. Wordlessly he turned and let Johnny pass him in the narrow hallway, then locked the gate and the heavy door after him. He led the way down the long hallway and turned into a small, dark kitchen. A fat girl who looked Polish got up without a word and left the room, closing the door behind herself.

The man reached over the sink and took down a half-filled gallon jug of red wine. He poured out two tea cups full and handed one to Johnny.

"How's the boy?" he asked.

"He's fine; doing it on his ear. Told me to tell you not to worry."

The man looked sour.

"Doing the book on his ear. Not to worry. I worry plenty," he said. "Goddamn it, I worry plenty."

"He's tough," Johnny said. "Plenty tough. And he's hoping to get a break."

"I'm hoping he gets a break, too," the man said. "Anyway, what can I do for you?"

"I want a room," Johnny said. "For about two weeks. Just a room, no bath. I won't be in much. Don't want or need to have it cleaned. Don't want anyone but myself in it. I won't be having any visitors."

"You leaving anything in the room?"

"This," Johnny indicated the suitcase. "Another bag some-time next week."

The man nodded.

"Won't nobody disturb them," he said, without curiosity.

Johnny took out his wallet.

"Won't be no charge," Piano said. "You said Patsy sent you."

Johnny nodded.

"Yeah, he sent me," he said. "But we're friends and I'd feel better if you let me pay you for the room. This is a sort of business arrangement and I can afford it."

The man grunted.

"O.K.," he said. "Ten bucks a week. I'll send the money in butts to the boy."

He stood up and beckoned Johnny to follow him.

It was a small, rectangular room on the second floor at the end of the hallway. The door was padlocked from the outside. There was a single, heavily curtained window and the furnishings were sparse.

"It'll do fine," Johnny said.

The man handed him a key.

"I got the only other one," he said. "You don't have to worry about leaving anything here. It'll be safe. I don't give out keys to the front door. You have to ring. But I'm always here and I don't care what time you come in. Doesn't matter. Only be careful..."

"No one will ever tail me here," Johnny said.

Again the man grunted. He turned, wordlessly, and padded off down the hallway.

Johnny went over to the dresser and pulled out the bottom drawer. The suitcase just fitted. A moment later and he closed the door of the room behind himself, turned and snapped the padlock. He put the key in his watch pocket before leaving the building.

On the way back downtown, he was tempted to stop off and have something to eat. But then he decided against it. He wanted to be back at Unger's in time to receive George Peatty's phone call. He'd tell George that everything was O.K. Tell him to show up for the big meeting on Monday night. The meeting at which they'd make the final arrangements.

He would be glad to get back to the East Thirty-first Street apartment.

He'd had a busy day.

❊CHAPTER VI❊

Randy Kennan sat in back of the wheel of the sedan, a newspaper held in front of his face. He hadn't long to wait. At exactly eight forty, the front door of the apartment house opened and Marvin Unger walked out and turned west, looking neither to right or to left. Randy gave him an extra minute or two after he had passed the corner and turned downtown. Then he climbed out of the car and entered the building.

Johnny had a cup of black coffee in his hand when he answered the soft knock on the door.

"Glad you got my message," he said, smiling at the other man and quickly stepping aside to let him enter.

Randy smiled back.

"Gotta 'nother cup?" he asked.

Johnny nodded and went into the kitchen. Randy followed him.

"What's the rub?" the cop asked. "I thought we planned the meet for tonight?"

"No rub," Johnny said. "It's just that I want to talk to you first—alone."

Randy took the cup of coffee Johnny held out and reached for a chair.

"Everything all right with the others?"

"Everything's set," Johnny said. "I just wanted to talk to you alone." He hesitated a second, watching Randy closely, and then went on.

"It's like this," he said. "When the cards are down, here's the way it stacks up. You and I are the ones who are really carrying the ball. And you are the only one I can actually count on. Not," he added quickly, seeing the suddenly startled look on the policeman's face, "not that the others aren't all right as far as they go. The trouble is, they just don't go far enough.

"Right now, Unger's out getting the five grand I'm going to need today to tie up the boys who are helping me out at the track. That's fine. We need Unger and that's why he's in. We need Big Mike, too, and we can count on him. He's old, he's tired and discouraged and God knows he probably has plenty of problems of his own. But he's invaluable to us and won't let us down. The same goes for Peatty."

He stopped then for a minute and refilled his cup.

"What's on your mind, kid?" Randy said. "We already been over all that."

"Right. We have," Johnny said. "But coming to Peatty, we come to another problem. Peatty's wife. As far as George goes, he knows what he has to do and he'll do it. We can trust him. But that business of his wife showing up still bothers me. Let me tell you exactly what happened after you guys left the other night."

For the next ten minutes Johnny talked and as he went over the details of the scene between himself and Sherry Peatty, Randy once or twice grinned widely. He didn't interrupt until Johnny was through talking.

"So what," he said at last. "The kid's got hot pants and George can't take care of her. That's all it amounts to. That and the fact that she's nosy."

"You may be right. On the other hand, the dame worries me. It's a little too pat."

"Well," Randy said, "you say she's going to show up at two o'clock? Right? You'll have all afternoon then to find out what it's all about. So you should kick? She may be a dizzy broad, but hell, Johnny, she's..."

"You miss the point," Johnny said. "She's going to show up,

but I don't think I'm going to find out anything. I don't even like the idea of her showing. In the first place, I got other things to do today. I gotta meet Unger at one thirty and pick up the dough. I got to spread that money around."

"What are you trying to tell me?" Randy said. "You mean you don't want to meet the girl? My God, Johnny, those years up the river must have done something to you after all. Anyone would take a crack..."

"You don't get the picture," Johnny said shortly. "In the first place, if you'd talked to her, you'd realize that she's wide open. Anybody can take a crack at her. I don't want to go into details; I just think I'm the wrong guy for the job. There's too much else on my mind."

"Another dame?" Randy said, looking up sharply.

"What it is doesn't matter," Johnny said. "Try and get the idea. I don't think I can handle her. On the other hand, you're a guy who has a reputation for handling broads. I'm suggesting that you be here when she shows up this afternoon. Play her along and see what you can learn. If she's up to something, we have to know. I can't tell you why, but for some reason I got the feeling something is sour with her."

Randy looked thoughtful for several moments before he spoke.

"You think Peatty is in on a double cross of some kind?"

"No. No, George wasn't putting on an act the other night. He was probably more surprised than we were when she showed up. But I can't get over the idea that she's up to something. Whatever it is, we have to know about it."

Randy got up from the chair and rattled the coffeepot. He put it down and then turned back to Johnny.

"And you say she'll be here at around two this afternoon? And that she likes Scotch?"

"Right. And Randy, remember one thing. She may be an oversexed little lush, but you have to handle her with kid gloves. She wants to be romanced, not raped. Probably gets enough of that at home."

Randy Kennan grunted.

"Well, boy," he said, "you don't have to tell me how to handle that kind of dame. Is there any booze in the joint?"

Johnny laughed.

"You forget whose joint it is?"

Randy smiled.

"Right," he said. "I'll pick up a couple of jugs and be back here at one thirty."

Johnny took the key off his ring.

"O.K.," he said. "Here's the key; I'll be gone. And whatever you do, get her the hell out of here by six, before Marvin gets home. And clean up after yourselves."

*　*　*　*　*

They arrived within fifteen minutes of each other, first the short, heavy-set one with the dead, half smoked cigar between thick over-red lips and with his sweat-stained, gray felt hat tipped on the back of his completely bald, round head. And then the little man with the thin consumptive body and the oversized ugly head which hung forward from his stringy neck and always looked as though it were about to drop off altogether.

They had walked through the barroom, nodding at the big man sitting on the stool as they passed through the doorway leading into the long narrow hall. Each one had gone to the last door down and knocked softly three times.

Val Cannon, his lean, wide-shouldered frame covered with a Chinese silk dressing gown, his silk clad ankles thrust into half slippers, had opened the door leading into the air conditioned apartment, himself. The three of them were alone and although Val had a Scotch and soda in his hand, he had not offered the others anything. He sat back, in a large leather club chair, his long legs crossed. The window of the room was closed and covered by a large pull curtain. Looking around at the modern, almost sparse furnishings, it was hard to tell whether it was a living room or an office.

The heavy-set man was speaking.

"So I talked with Steiner," he said. "Leo knew him, all right. In fact, like I figured, he owes Leo dough. Quite a chunk of dough."

"It figures," Val said. "Go on."

"Leo couldn't tell me much, but he did give me this. This cop, this guy Keenan, told him, Leo, that he was expecting to come into a considerable chunk of dough by the end of the month. Well, I had Leo get a hold of him on the phone and put on the pressure. The way it ended up was the cop says he absolutely won't be able to pay off until the end of the week. He didn't make a flat promise, but Leo got the feeling that he would get his dough before next Monday."

Val nodded, thoughtfully. He lifted the glass to his thin lips and took a sip. He turned to the other man.

"So?"

The thin man tensed, seemed suddenly to stand at attention.

"It was easy," he said. "Easy. I got hold the janitor. The joint belongs to a guy named Marvin Unger. He's some kind of clerk down at the Municipal Building. Been living there since the place opened up several years back. He's a bachelor and lives alone. Never has any guests what the janitor can remember. No dames. A straight-laced guy."

"Now about..."

"Getting to that," the thin man said. "He don't play the neighborhood bookie; don't hang out in the bars. Gets the Wall Street Journal so I guess maybe the market is his weakness. Outside of that, I couldn't find out nothing."

"The others?"

The little man shrugged.

"God only knows," he said. He walked over to a desk and took a cigarette from a box. The heavy-set man took a silver lighter from his pocket and held it to the half smoked cigar.

"How about you, Val?"

Cannon leaned forward in his chair.

"I got a little," he said. "Saw the girl yesterday. She's going back again this afternoon. Seems a guy staying in the place is making a play for her. Guy's name is Johnny Clay. I checked on him. He got out of the big house a short time back. A smalltime punk who did a jolt on a larceny charge. I'll have a run-down on him in a day or so. Seems to be the leader of the mob, if it is a mob.

"All she knows now—and this she got from her husband and not the Clay guy—is that they're definitely going to knock over the track office. How they plan to do it, and when they plan to do it, is anybody's guess. But she's sure they will make the pitch. Her husband's a cashier out at the track and he's mixed up in it. You can bet there are a couple of more inside men. What part the cop's going to take, I wouldn't know. That's one angle I can't figure. Also this guy, Unger. I can't figure him, unless maybe he's putting up the nut money. One thing is sure, this is no professional mob. So far the only one who seems to have any sort of record is this Clay guy and he's strictly small time."

The fat man grunted.

"Nobody planning to knock off the track is small time."

Val went on, looking irritated.

"The best guess I can make at this point is that it will be along toward the end of the week. One thing, we can probably keep a pretty accurate tab on what they do so that we'll have a little warning as to when they make their move. That's all we got to know. There is just one chance in about fifty thousand that they'll get away with it, although I still can't see how it figures. On the other hand, that guy Peatty must know all the handicaps and if he's still going in on the deal, they may have some gimmick which I can't figure."

He stopped then and stood up. Without saying anything more he left the room and came back a couple of minutes later with a fresh drink in his hand. He continued talking where he had left off.

"One thing is for sure," he said. "Any move we make will have to be after it's all over and done with. For my dough, I don't think they've got one chance in a million of getting away with it. And it's a sure bet that none of us want to be seen around Long Island on the day they try this caper. If by any god damned chance they do do it, and do get away with it, this town is going to be hotter than the rear end of a jet plane and for a long time to come."

The little man squashed out his cigarette and smiled.

"It'll be hot," he said. "How about a drink, Val?"

Cannon stared at him.

"We're partners in getting money," he said, "not in spending it. Go out to the bar and buy your own god damned drink."

*****

Walking east to Broadway where he'd get the subway which would take him down to Penn Station, from where he in turn would get the train going out to Long Island, George, Peatty began to think over the last twenty-four hours.

At eleven o'clock on Sunday morning, freshly shaved and wearing a white shirt and a blue serge suit with polished black shoes, he'd been standing hatless in a delicatessen store at the corner of Broadway and One Hundred and Ninth Street.

He'd ordered three hard rolls, which he liked, and a half dozen French doughnuts, which Sherry liked. Then he'd asked for two pint containers of coffee, with sugar and cream. He saw a jar of sour pickles and ordered that as well. It would be nice later in the day.

George was going through his usual Sunday morning ritual. He always got up first, showered, shaved and dressed and went down to the delicatessen for his and Sherry's breakfast. By the time he had picked up the morning papers and taken a short walk along the Drive before returning, Sherry would be up and waiting.

He saw a can of imported sardines and was about to order that also when he suddenly reflected that he probably wouldn't have enough change to pay for it if he wanted to pick up the Sunday newspapers.

Tucking the bag under his arm as he was leaving, he began thinking how nice it was going to be to really have money.

Money to burn. They'd live in a hotel, he figured. Sherry would like that. And on Sunday instead of getting a breakfast from the nearest delicatessen, they'd order it up from room service.

They could spend the day laying around in bed reading the papers and doing other interesting things.

George thought he knew what Sherry wanted; all it took was the money to make it possible.

He hurried home; thinking of Sherry gave him an irresistible desire to see her.

The note had been waiting for him, pinned by a thumbtack to the outside of the apartment door. One of Sherry's girl friends was sick and had called to ask Sherry to stop by. The note didn't name the girl friend.

George Peatty had breakfast alone.

In fact, George had spent the rest of the afternoon and most of the evening alone. Along about six o'clock he had begun to worry a little and he'd called a couple of numbers where he thought she might be. But he'd been unable to trace her.

By the time she did finally get in, around ten o'clock, he'd been so glad to see her that he hadn't even asked where she'd been. They'd had a couple of drinks together after Sherry told him she'd already eaten. And then they'd gone to bed.

It had been like that other night.

He hadn't been able to understand why she had been so curious about the stick-up plans. But in order to satisfy her, and also for other more personal reasons, he'd finally told her a little. Not the exact day, but just that it wouldn't be more than another week or ten days. And then he had fallen asleep.

It was only now, the next day, as he was on his way to work, that he began to wonder. That certain, persistent thought kept crossing his mind and refused to go away. He tried not to think about it, tried to drive it from his mind, but it refused to go away.

When he got off the subway at Penn Station he looked up at the clock and saw that he had about eighteen minutes in which to catch his train. He had a splitting headache.

Turning, he went up the ramp and out onto Thirty-Fourth Street. A moment later and he found the bar.

For the first time that he could remember he ordered a drink of straight whiskey before noon.

By the time he had finished his second drink he realized that he had missed his train. George Peatty was not a man who had often become drunk. By the same token, he was a man who very rarely had faced the truth and recognized it as such, if the truth should happen to be unpleasant.

Standing there at the bar, with two shots of straight rye under his belt on an otherwise almost empty stomach, George suddenly no longer refused to face the little bothersome thought which had persisted in annoying him on the way downtown in the subway.

Sherry had lied about seeing a sick friend. There was simply no doubt about it; she had lied. He realized now, in thinking it over, that he had known all along that she was lying. But he had been too cowardly to face the reality of proving it to himself.

Looking up, George suddenly beckoned the bartender.

"Another shot," he said. And then, without fully realizing he was going to do so, he added, "And I am not going to work today."

The bartender looked at him skeptically from under heavy, overhanging brows, but turned nevertheless and reached for the bottle. He was used to them all—every kind of a screw ball that there was. The worst of them, he usually got before noon.

Between his third and fourth drink, George went to a telephone and called the track. He told them that he wouldn't be in, that he was home sick and expected to be all right the following day.

Then he went back to the bar and ordered another drink. There was no point in kidding himself. Sherry was a tramp. She was a tramp and she was a liar.

She'd come home last night with lipstick smeared all over her face. Her breath reeked of liquor. She had been with no sick girl friend. She'd been with some man, lapping up whiskey and

God only knows what else.

George ordered another drink.

He wasn't, at the moment, curious as to who the man might be. It was enough to finally admit that Sherry was running around with other men. But the fact, once he was willing to accept the truth, was irrefutable.

At once George began to feel sorry for Sherry and to blame himself. If she was running with other men, it could only mean that he had failed her. George felt a tear come to the corner of his eye and he was about to beckon the waiter to refill his glass. It was then that he caught sight of his face in the mirror behind the stacks of pyramided bottles. In a split second he sobered up completely.

What kind of god damned idiot was he? Good God, here it was the most important week in his life and he was standing at a public bar getting drunk. He should have been at the track. The last thing in the world he should have done was to have failed to follow the usual routine of his days.

Quickly he turned from the bar, not bothering to pick up his change. Well, it was too late now to make the track, but at least he would go out and get some food into his stomach and some hot coffee. Then he would go to a movie and take it easy. He fully realized how essential it was that he be completely sober before evening.

Tonight was the big meeting. And he, George, wanted to get there a little before the meeting. He wanted to talk to Johnny alone for a minute or two before the others arrived. He wanted to assure Johnny that they would have nothing to worry about as far as he, George, was concerned.

* * * * *

Watching her through half closed eyes as she lay back on the bed, her arms spread wide, her breasts slowly rising and falling with her deep breathing and the long lashes closed over her own eyes, he thought, my God, she's really beautiful.

It was a nice thought.

He pulled deeply on the cigarette and then slowly exhaled, still looking at her through the veil of smoke.

His next thought wasn't so nice.

A tramp. A god damned tramp. A push over. Jesus—it hadn't taken an hour. Less than sixty minutes from the time she had walked through that door until they were in bed together.

That was the trouble. She was beautiful. She was a bum. He was nuts about her.

For a minute he wondered if he was blowing his top. Anybody had told him, Randy Kennan, that he could run into a girl, especially some other guy's wife, talk to her for a few minutes, end up in bed with her and then convince himself he was half in love with her and he'd have said the guy was simply plain crazy.

Randy was a cop and he had the psychology of a cop. There were good women and bad women. This one there was no doubt at all about. She was bad.

And by God if he hadn't gone and fallen for her—hook, line and sinker.

Maybe it was because he was bad, too.

Suddenly he threw the cigarette into the far corner of the room without bothering to butt it. It landed in a shower of sparks. He leaned down across her and found her slightly parted lips. They felt like crushed grapes under the pressure of his hungry mouth.

She didn't open her eyes but in a moment she moaned slightly and then her arms went up and over his shoulders.

It was exactly five-fifteen when Randy finally got back into his clothes. He poked his head into the bathroom as he finished pulling on his coat.

"So I'll call you tomorrow, honey," he said. "Sorry I can't wait now, but I just have to report in within the next fifteen minutes. If I don't call in there'll be hell to pay and I don't want to call from here."

"You run on," Sherry told him. "I'll be out of here in another ten minutes myself. I want to be back home anyway by the time

George gets in tonight."

She looked up from where she was kneeling, pulling on a shoe, and blew him a kiss across the top of her overturned palm. Randy twisted his mouth in a smile. And then he was gone.

Pulling on her second shoe, Sherry realized that she'd have to hurry if she was to keep her appointment with Val Cannon. She had arranged to meet him in a cocktail lounge on the upper East Side at exactly five-thirty. Val wouldn't be inclined to wait if she was late.

Suddenly it occurred to her that she didn't really care whether he waited or not.

There was a startled look on her face as the idea hit her. It was the first time in months that she had become even slightly indifferent to Val and to what Val might do.

And then her mind went back to Randy. Randy Kennan. A cop.

My God, what was wrong with her that she never seemed able to resist falling for heels? And there was no doubt about it; she had fallen for Randy. The thing had hit her as suddenly as it had hit him.

Putting on her lipstick in front of the bathroom mirror, she made no effort to hurry. If Val waited for her, well and good. If he didn't, it wouldn't make the slightest difference.

She then decided that even if he did wait, he would learn nothing further as far as the track stick-up was concerned. At the thought, she couldn't help smiling. She had, in fact, learned nothing herself. She and that handsome six foot two Irishman had spent the afternoon discussing much more personal problems.

Carefully she wiped up after herself and dusted the powder off the washbasin. She threw several dirty pieces of kleenex into the toilet bowl and then flushed it.

She was careful to see that the door was left unlatched, as Randy had instructed her to do. The keys were lying on the table in the living room.

She took the elevator down to the ground floor and hurried

from the building. Looking neither to right nor left, she started east.

George Peatty, stepping from the curb on the opposite side of the street, suddenly stopped with one foot in midair. His face became deathly pale and for a moment he thought he might faint. And then, like a man in a slow motion picture, his foot again found the ground and he stepped back on the curb.

As he slowly followed his wife from a half a block's distance, there was but a single thought in his shocked mind.

"So that was why Johnny didn't beat her up."

He would have followed her into the subway, but he had to duck into a nearby doorway instead. The tears were running down his face and people were beginning to look at him. Even George himself didn't know whether it was self-pity or hatred which caused those tears.

✸{CHAPTER VII}✸

The temptation was almost irresistible. Marvin Unger was not a man who was usually bothered by temptation. Facing a problem, he invariably approached it coldly and scientifically. On the basis of straight reasoning, he would make his decision, and once that decision had been made, he would abide by it.

Now, at ten-thirty on Saturday morning, as he paced back and forth in the small living room of the apartment, he was suddenly undergoing a completely foreign sensation. He had already made up his mind that it would be not only unrewarding, but possibly downright foolhardy, to be at the race track that afternoon. Certainly his radio, as well as the evening newspapers, would give him all the information he needed to satisfy his curiosity. There was every possible reason for him to stay as far from the track as he could.

And yet, at this very moment, as the sun streaked through the dirty pane of the window and fell across the floor at his feet, he had this almost irresistible desire to leave the apartment and go out to Long Island. He wanted to watch—from, of course, a safe distance. For a moment, he tried to rationalize the thing. Perhaps, it would really be safest if he did go to the track. At least, in that case, should something go wrong, should the plan fail, he would have ample warning. Even as he thought about it, his thin mouth twisted in a bitter smile.

If the plan were to fail, all the warning in the world wouldn't do him any good. It would be just a case of hours before he would be picked up. Without money, the money which only the successful completion of the robbery would supply, he would be in no position to make a getaway in any case.

Once more he decided that being at the track was an unnecessary risk. Certainly it would be pointless. The radio would let him know what was taking place. Once more looking at the clock over the mantel, he made a quick calculation. He would have approximately six and a half hours to wait.

The Canarsie Stakes would be run around four-thirty that afternoon.

Six and a half hours! And then it would all be over. Well, that is it would be almost all over. There would be the meeting that night, in this very apartment, of course. The meeting at which the money would be split up. After that—well, after that, thank God, he'd be through with them. He'd never see one of them again.

The last week had brought considerable changes into Unger's plans. At first, when Sherry Peatty had been found at the door, he'd seriously regretted having gotten himself mixed up in the thing in the first place. He had started to realize all the possible things wrong with Johnny's scheme. And he had started doubting whether it would actually be successful.

Then, later, after they had gotten together and gone over the final details, he once more became optimistic. His faith had been revived. But, simultaneous with his renewed faith in the robbery itself, he had gradually begun to realize the fundamental weakness in the entire operation.

They'd get away with the robbery, of that he was fairly sure. Johnny had really worked it out to perfection. Yes, that part would go through fine. But, sooner or later, the police would crack the case. Unger had been around courts and police work for enough years to realize that they would have to be caught eventually. The very character of the men involved in the scheme made such an eventuality inevitable.

There was, first of all, Peatty. A weak character; a man ruled entirely by his frustrated relationship to his wife. And the wife herself was certainly a woman not to be trusted.

And then there was Big Mike, the bartender. A man who had never had money, who had always fought his battle on the fringes of need and poverty. Big Mike could be counted upon to do the wrong things once he came into his share of the loot. He wouldn't stop betting the horses—the chances are he'd over bet. And he'd make a splash; buy a new house, a new car. He'd show his prosperity at once.

It would be simply a matter of time until the Pinkertons, or the insurance detectives, or even the municipal police themselves, got around to Big Mike. Yes, those two, Mike and Peatty, were the essential weaknesses in the plan. The only difficulty, and this Unger realized full well, was that Mike and Peatty also were essential to the success of the robbery.

Understanding all of this, Marvin Unger had also reached another conclusion. First, the robbery would be successful. Secondly, sooner or later one of the members of the gang would be picked up and would, without doubt, crack under pressure. Third, other members of the gang would be known and arrested.

The conclusion was obvious.

Marvin Unger must collect his share at once and disappear. After all, he would be in no worse a position than an absconding bank teller. And certainly a good many bank tellers had been able to successfully abscond.

To begin with, he'd have somewhere near a half a million dollars. And, barring accident, he would have a certain amount of time in which to make his getaway. It was the only safe and sane plan.

Marvin Unger had, upon reaching this decision, at once acted accordingly.

He had arranged to take a two week's vacation from his job down at the courthouse, starting on the following Monday. His bags were already packed and checked in at Grand Central. His ticket to Montreal and his Pullman reservation on the midnight train were in his wallet. His plans were made, and were, he hoped, without flaw.

From Montreal, where he would take on a new identity, he would fly to the West Coast. And from there he would again enter the States, ending up in Los Angeles. A new name and a new life and plenty of money to start out fresh on. If by some miracle his name was never mentioned in connection with the robbery, well then it would be merely a case of Marvin Unger, unimportant clerk, having disappeared during his regular summer vacation. Having neither close relatives or intimate friends, the most cursory of investigations would be made.

On the other hand, should he finally be connected with the stick-up, he would long since have passed into oblivion.

There was little now to be done. Fortunately, Johnny Clay had changed his own plans and left the apartment two days before for some secret hideaway of his own. It had given Marvin the opportunity to arrange the details of his runout in complete privacy. He had done everything himself. He was sure that there was not a single print of Clay's left in the place. Nor one personal possession which might be traced to him. He had even sold to the secondhand store around on Third Avenue everything of any possible value.

It suddenly occurred to him that among the possessions he had parted with, was the portable radio. The radio he had intended using to hear reports of the robbery.

Marvin Unger looked up at the empty spot on the shelf where the radio used to stand.

Once more he smiled, wryly. He got to his feet, reached for his light Panama hat and went to the door.

Twenty minutes later and he was crowding onto the first of the special trains leaving Penn Station for the race track.

At least he would be cagey. He would stay well away from the clubhouse. But from where he would be, down in the stands, he would certainly be able to see and hear everything that took place.

After all, a man who had several hundred thousand dollars or better riding had a right to witness the race.

Looking across the kitchen table at Mary, he blew across the cup of black coffee he held in one shaking hand. Big Mike spoke in a low, bitter growl.

* * * * *

"A tramp," he said. "A damned little tramp! Four-thirty it was when she came in. Reeking of vomit and gin and with her dress all torn down the front. My own daughter. I never thought I'd live to see the day..."

His wife lifted her faded blue eyes and stared at him.

"And what do you expect the child to do of a Friday night if she don't have a date?" she asked.

"A date!"

For a moment Big Mike felt like getting up and slapping her. Slapping her across the face and then going into the bedroom and pulling Patti out and giving her the whaling that she deserved.

"Can't she have a date with decent boys? Does she have to hang around every scum in this neighborhood? What's the matter with the child—God knows she's been brought up proper."

"She's been brought up in this neighborhood," Mary said. "With the rest of the scum. What do you expect? What can you expect?"

For a minute then, Mike stared at her before he dropped his eyes.

She's right, he thought. Yes, God knows she's right. It wasn't the child's fault. Patti was a good girl. Remembering how she had come in, her discontented mouth smeared with lipstick, her clothes torn and dirty, still sick from the swill she'd been drinking, he blamed himself. What could be expected of a child brought up in the slums, never meeting anyone but the boys from the neighborhood?

She's seventeen, he thought, and she's never really had anything. This is all she's known.

Mike took a deep breath, sighed and drank from the cup. Well, after today it would be different. It still wasn't too late.

They'd move out of this stinking neighborhood; get out to Long Island and have a small house and a yard in one of the nicer suburbs. Patti could go to a good school and she could have new clothes and money in her pocketbook. She'd be able to meet nice boys, from nice homes. It was just a case of money, and soon he'd have the money.

Of course the girl had been talking about quitting school and getting a job. But once he had the dough, he'd get her over that nonsense. Even if he had to get her a roadster and give her an allowance, he'd get her over that sort of talk.

With money, she'd meet the right boys and then she'd be a good girl and they could stop worrying about her.

It would be easier on all of them. He wouldn't have to take the long train ride twice each day; he'd even give up playing the horses. Hell, he wouldn't have to play them any more. He'd have all the money he needed.

As he stood up and reached for the jacket hanging over the back of his chair, Big Mike began to consider the stick-up almost in the light of a holy mission.

It never once occurred to him that if he hadn't played the horses he would have had enough money to have moved out into the suburbs a long time ago. It never occurred to him that this pretty little hot-eyed daughter of his would have been exactly the same, irrespective of what school she went to or what boys she dated.

His face tired and drawn from a sleepless night, he reached down and patted Mary on the arm.

"Well, cheer up, Mother," he said. "I can't tell you about it now, but things are going to be different. Very different—and soon."

She looked up at him and there was that old, soft expression of abiding affection that she always had had, right from the very beginning.

"Have you got yourself a good one today, Mike?" she asked and her mouth smiled at him.

"'Tis no horse," he said, "that's changing our luck. Just you keep your chin up and wait. There'll be a change all right." He leaned over and brushed her cheek with his lips as he turned to leave.

"And don't wait supper," he said. "I'll be late. Got an appointment and won't be in until sometime near midnight. Don't you wait up and don't you worry."

He slammed the door behind himself as he left the tenement. Already he was feeling better about Patti. The girl had good and decent stuff in her, underneath it all. After all, wasn't she his own flesh and blood? She just needed a chance.

Looking up at the clock in the hardware store as he passed on his way toward the subway, he saw that it was half past ten. Well, in another six hours the thing would take place which would give her her chance; which would solve all of his problems. He smiled quietly to himself and in spite of the sleepless night and the natural nervousness he felt as a result of this final tension, he began to feel better. The excitement was still with him and, in fact, was beginning to grow, but he was all right now.

He knew what he had to do and he was ready to do it. He wasn't worried. Excited or not, when the time came, he'd go through with his end of it.

For the first time in as long as he could remember, he didn't stop at the newsstand on the corner and pick up a racing form.

He left the subway at Penn Station, but instead of going downstairs to the Long Island division, he went up to the main lobby. He found the bank of steel lockers exactly where Johnny had told him they would be.

Carefully he looked around after locating number 809. He saw no one he knew.

Mike took the key and inserted it and turned. He pulled the door open.

It was a florist's box, about three feet long, twelve inches wide and eight inches deep. It was beautifully wrapped and tied with a large red ribbon. There was only one thing wrong with it. It weighed about twenty-five pounds.

Walking to the train, Mike saw a number of men whom he knew. Some were fellow employees at the track; others steady customers. He nodded; said hello a couple of times. He tried not to look self-conscious.

On the train, going out to Long Island, he sat on a seat toward the end of the second car, next to the window, and he stared through it without seeing a thing. He had made the trip a thousand times, several thousand times in fact, and he'd always hated it. But today it didn't bother him at all. Somehow or other, anxious as he was to get to the track and to get the thing over with, he found himself enjoying and relishing each moment of contemplation.

Shortly before twelve o'clock, along with several hundred other track and concession employees as well as a handful of diehards who always arrived long before the first race was scheduled to start, he left the train and started for the gates.

The employees' dressing room was on the west, or street side, of the second floor of the clubhouse. It was sandwiched in between the main business office, which occupied the corner position, and the long narrow room which held the small cubbyholes of the endless cashier's cages. The entrance to the locker room faced the lobby and consisted of a blank door without an outside knob.

The door was always opened from within by an employee who had entered the adjacent office with a key and had passed from that office into the locker room and released the spring lock. A third door led from the locker room to the long aisle behind the cashiers' cages. It was for this reason that the entrance door was blank—a safety measure to prohibit any one from coming in by way of the main lobby without first passing through the main business office, once the races started.

There were a dozen men already in the room when Mike entered. He went at once to his locker, one of those nearest the washstands. He opened the door and put the flower box in, standing it on end. It barely fitted. He took his hat off, unconsciously dusting the brim. Then he removed his suit coat and snapped a pair of sleeve bands on his arms. He took out a fresh white bar jacket.

No one had commented on the flower box.

"It's a beautiful day, Michael," Willy Harrigan, a stick man at the bar in the grandstands, said, looking over at him. "Should be a big crowd!"

Big Mike nodded.

"Who do you like, boy?" he asked. It was his inevitable opening gambit and he spoke the words without thinking and also without remembering that for the first time in years, he had arrived at the track without having made a bet.

"I like the favorite in the big race," Willy told him. "But I don't like the price. No, the price will go all to pieces before the race. Nobody can beat that horse. Nobody."

Big Mike nodded.

"You're right, lad," he said. "They can't beat Black Lightning!"

"But the price," Willy said. "I can't afford the odds. So I'm betting on Bright Sun."

Big Mike nodded sagaciously.

"A smart bet, Willy," he said. "Don't think he can possibly beat Black Lightning, but what the hell. No point in going down on a horse that'll pay a lot less than even money."

"That's the way I see it," Willy said.

Frank Raymond, cashier at Big Mike's bar, laughed as he struggled with his bow tie.

"You guys kill me," he said. "You figure one horse is going to win, so you go right ahead and bet another horse. What the hell's the difference what price a nag pays, just so he wins?"

"But less than even money," Mike objected.

"I'd rather get two fifty back for two dollars, than lose the two," Frank said.

"You ain't ever going to get rich that way."

"You ain't ever going to get rich any way you play 'em," Frank said.

"Right you are, Mister," Mike said.

He smiled secretly to himself as he left the dressing room. No, none of them would get rich; none of them except himself, Big Mike. And before this day was over, he'd have it made. There was no doubt in Mike's mind about the success of the stick-up. No doubt about their getting away with it.

Behind the bar, beginning to arrange the bottles and get the glassware out, he felt fresh as a daisy, in spite of his lack of sleep. He'd completely lost his nervousness. He was ready and waiting. Completely calm and under control.

It was a peculiar thing, but for the first time in all the years he had been tending bar at the track, he failed to experience that odd sense of excitement which had never failed to affect him before the races started. It was going to be the biggest day in his life, and for the first time, the strange, subtle undercurrent of tension and expectancy which the track and its crowds always gave him, was missing.

Today Mike knew that he had the winner.

He hadn't told her. In spite of everything she had done, every trick and every subtle maneuver, George still hadn't told her. Everything else, yes. Who was in on the deal, how it was going to be pulled.

* * * * *

But not when. Not the day.

Hours before dawn broke across the eastern sky and the sun slanted through the bedroom window to wake her up, Sherry Peatty knew. Knew it was going to be this day. Finding the gun, probably more than anything else, was the tip off.

George had gone out on Friday night and told her not to wait up; that he'd be late. But she'd still been up when he came in just before twelve o'clock. At once she'd noticed his peculiarly furtive attitude. He asked her to mix a drink, which in itself was unusual. She hadn't questioned him, but had gone at once into the kitchen. He had moved off to the bedroom. Instead of starting to mix the drink, she'd given him only a minute or two, and then followed him. He'd been standing at the dresser and he whirled quickly as she entered the room. The gun was still in his hand and apparently he'd been about to put it into the top bureau drawer where he kept his shirts.

"What in the world have you got there?" she asked.

He blushed, started to say something. But she went to him at once and reached for it. He brushed her hand away then and told her not to touch it.

"My God, George," she said then. "Don't tell me you're going to actually be in on the stick-up yourself." She looked at him with wide eyes, unbelievingly.

It wasn't that at all, he told her. But he felt safer with the gun. The gun was for afterward, once they had divided the money up.

"But I don't understand," she said. "Is it that you don't trust the others? You think someone's going to try..."

"I trust them," he said, almost too quickly. "I trust them, all right. Only, it's going to be a lot of money. And it isn't only us that will be in it. Johnny's got two or three outside men, hoodlums, working on the thing."

"You trust Johnny, don't you?" she asked.

For a moment then, as she mentioned his name, he seemed to turn away and his neck grew red.

"As much as I trust anyone," he told her, shortly.

She wanted to know where he got the gun; wanted to know why he brought it home. Asked if it wasn't dangerous, just having it around. But he was evasive. He told her he didn't want her worrying about it.

Finally she asked him outright if he brought it home because they were going to pull the job immediately.

He protested then, protested too much and she knew that the next day must be the day.

As she had fallen asleep, she was still surprised, however, that George had gotten hold of a revolver. For a fleeting moment she wondered if he could possibly have any suspicion of her relationship with Val Cannon. Could possibly have guessed what she had told Val. But she brushed the idea aside.

There was no doubt but what George had been acting strange the last few days; tense, even short and surly with her. She put it down to a bad case of nerves. She knew that as the time for the stick-up approached, he would of necessity be highly nervous and upset.

Still and all, the gun didn't quite fit into the picture. George wasn't the type to carry a gun. In fact, she doubted very seriously if he had ever as much as shot off a gun in his entire life.

George Peatty himself had slept badly. He had, in fact, been sleeping badly for about a week. It wasn't only the robbery which worried him. There was the business of Sherry. First her showing up that night of the first meeting. Then, seeing her coming out of Unger's apartment that following Monday at dusk.

Something was going on, and George didn't know what it was. He had, as casually as possible, mentioned Sherry to Johnny a couple of times lately. But Johnny had been noncommittal. Certainly in no way had he indicated that he had seen her that Monday afternoon.

Just why he had picked up the gun, George couldn't even say to himself. He only knew that suddenly, around the middle of the week, he remembered a friend of his who had a collection of revolvers and rifles. He'd never paid much attention to it as he had no interest in either guns or the purposes for which they were used. But he remembered this friend and then the next thing, he'd looked him up. Called him on the telephone and just about invited himself over for a visit.

He'd given the man a long cock-and-bull story about taking a vacation up in the Canadian woods. Wanted to take a gun along with him as he'd be sleeping out in the car nights.

The man had offered to loan him a rifle or a shotgun, but George had asked for a revolver. Said he'd feel better with one in the glove compartment of his car. His friend had demurred, but finally he'd loaned George the revolver. He'd had to instruct George about how it worked.

It was a small, .32 automatic and as his friend explained about it, George couldn't help but be secretly amused. Here he was, he thought, a member of a mob which was about to pull just about the most daring stick-up in the history of crime, and someone had to show him how to load and unload a gun.

Sherry was up before George and half dressed as he threw the sheet from his body and started to climb out of bed.

"We're out of everything," she said, speaking over her shoulder as she started for the bathroom. "You get shaved and dressed and I'll run downstairs and pick up some coffee and rolls. You want anything else besides?"

"Might get a paper," George said.

"Newspaper or a scratch sheet?"

"Newspaper."

George sat on the edge of his bed, a scrawny scarecrow in his faded striped shorts. He smoked a cigarette as he waited for Sherry to get through in the bathroom. He coughed several times and butted out the cigarette, mentally reminding himself that he was going to cut out smoking before he'd had his morning coffee. At once he began to think of the plans for the day, of what would be happening out at the track this afternoon.

Unconsciously, he reached for another cigarette and lit it.

Sherry came out of the bathroom looking fresh and lovely, even without makeup. She took a scarf from one of the bureau drawers and tied it around her neck. She didn't bother with a hat or a jacket. She was wearing light peach-colored slacks and a turtle-neck sweater, her small feet thrust into huaraches. She looks, George thought, about seventeen.

"Money," she said.

"On the dresser, baby."

She took a couple of bills from George's wallet and blew him a casual kiss as she turned and left.

"Back in a jiff," she said.

George got up and went into the bathroom. He walked over to the mirror above the sink and leaned forward to stare at his face. He half opened his mouth and rubbed one hand down the side of his cheek, blinked his bloodshot, faded blue eyes several times. The stubble on his chin was very light and he could have gotten away without shaving. But he reached over and unhooked the door to the medicine cabinet and took out his safety razor, the moth-eaten shaving brush and a jar of shaving cream.

He nicked himself on the chin and on the side of his neck and swore under his breath each time. After he was through and had washed off the razor under the hot water faucet, he tore two tiny pieces from the roll of toilet paper and put them over the cuts to stop the bleeding.

Going back into the bedroom, he opened the bureau drawer to take out some clean underwear and a shirt. Suddenly he remembered the gun.

Quickly glancing at the bedroom door, with almost a guilty expression in his eyes, he reached under the shirts and took out the automatic. He held it at an awkward angle, pointed down toward his feet, and experimentally flipped off the safety catch. He closed one eye and lifting the weapon straight out in front of himself, sighted along it.

His face took on a hard, tough expression and he gritted his teeth. There was something almost pathetically comical about his entire pose.

"Drop the gun, Louie!"

George swung around as Sherry spoke the words from the door. Her face was convulsed with silent laughter as she stood there with the paper bag holding their breakfast, under her arm.

The gun fell from George's hand and struck the floor with a heavy thud.

"Jesus Christ, Sherry," he said. "I didn't hear you. Why..."

"Pick it up, George," she said. "My God, if you're going to be a two gun killer, you better keep a little more on your toes. I slammed the door when I came in and you never even heard me."

George blushed and reached down to pick up the revolver.

"Pour the coffee," he said. "I'll be right in."

George caught the same train from Penn Station that carried Big Mike out to the track. He saw Mike as the other man climbed aboard and he purposely walked a couple of cars down before finding a seat. He had left the morning paper with Sherry and hadn't bothered to buy a second one to read during the trip out to the Island.

Instead, he sat thinking. He was thinking about figures. As near as George could calculate, there would be approximately two million dollars in the offices of the track officials that afternoon at the end of the day, barring accident. That would include profits on the pari-mutuel betting, the break-, age money, the tax moneys from the mutuel machines, and the money from the concessions—the restaurant, the bars, hot dog stands, program venders—and there would be the take from the entrance fee windows of the race track itself.

George knew that cash was never allowed to collect at any point around the track. The mutuel windows turned over their surplus at the end of each race to messengers who brought it to the main office. What was needed for the payoff, was estimated at the end of the race and certain sums to meet the obligations were rushed to each pay-off cashier.

At the end of the day, all of the money was bundled up and an armored car swung by and guards picked up the entire take. Less than a few thousand dollars at most would be left in the safe at the track overnight.

As near as George could estimate, the total amount picked up by the armed cars was roughly equivalent to the total handle of the day. It had to work out that way, considering entrance fees and concession money. Figuring this way, at the end of the big race, the Canarsie Stakes, there should be at least something better than a million and a half dollars in the till. Saturday was always the biggest day of the week, and this particular Saturday, with the stakes running, and at the end of July, was sure to attract a record crowd.

Johnny's planning had certainly been smart. At the end of the day, there wouldn't be one chance in ten million of getting their hands on that money.

George knew that the armored car arrived around five o'clock and parked just opposite the main entrance to the clubhouse. Two men stayed in that car, one at the wheel and the other handling a machine gun from a turret on the top of the vehicle. Two others entered the offices, each fully armed. There would be the Pinkertons lining the path from the office to the door. There would be the two detectives who were on constant duty in the main offices, where the money itself was collected.

No, once that armored car showed, a stick-up would be impossible.

Thinking about it, thinking of what Johnny was planning to do, George shuddered.

Jesus, the guy had guts. He had to admit it. He not only had the brains to plan it, but he had guts to carry it out. It was going to take a particularly rare brand of courage to walk into that office, alone, and face those armed Pinkertons.

George looked at his wrist watch as the train pulled along the platform near the track. He unconsciously noted that the train, as always, was right on time.

He spoke to no one as he made his way to the clubhouse.

Another four hours.

* * * * *

Randy Kennan went on duty at eight o'clock on Saturday morning. He was on for a straight twelve hour trick. Patroling, first up one street and then down the next. Routine.

Climbing into the black and white prowl car, he offered up a fervent prayer that it would stay routine. But no matter what happened, no matter if there were half a dozen murders and a race riot on his beat, he knew what he had to do and he was prepared to do it.

Fortunately, things started out quiet and they stayed that way during the morning hours. A couple of early morning drunks, a fight over on Columbus Avenue. A speeding ticket and a woman who'd lost her kid while she was in shopping.

At twelve-thirty, Randy called in and told the desk that he

was going to have lunch. He'd be out of the car for not more than a half hour. And then, at one o'clock, back behind the wheel, he once more reported in. There was nothing stirring.

At two o'clock, Randy pulled over in front of a drugstore on West Sixty-first Street near Broadway. He left the engine running and got out of the car, leaving the radio on so that he'd be able to hear it.

He went into the drugstore and entered a phone booth. He didn't have to look up the number. In a moment he had the desk sergeant at the precinct house. He didn't even try to disguise his voice. He knew that it wouldn't be recognized. The sergeant was used to hearing him over the short-wave set. Quickly he told the sergeant that he was Lieutenant O'Malley's brother-in-law, out at Shirley, Long Island.

"The Lieutenant's wife, my sister, has suddenly been taken sick," he said. "We got no phone out here. Wish you'd try and get word to the Lieutenant. I think he should come on out."

And then he hung up. A moment later he was back in the car and pulling away from the curb. He hoped that it would work.

Lieutenant O'Malley was his direct superior and he knew that they had no phone. He'd been a guest out at O'Malley's beach house several times himself.

It might work and it might not. There was always the chance that O'Malley would check back with the Suffolk police and try and find out what was the matter. On the other hand there was an equally good chance that O'Malley, given the message, would ask to be excused from duty and would rush out to see for himself.

If it happened that way, it would be just so much to the good. Then, in case there was a call for Randy between three and five o'clock, O'Malley wouldn't be on duty and his replacement wouldn't be too sure when he failed to contact Randy Kennan's prowl car. Unless it was something really hot, they'd just assume that Randy's radio was broken and he didn't get the call. And they'd send someone else out on it.

O'Malley, who made the rounds himself in another car and

checked up on Randy and the rest of the men in his district, was about the only one who was sufficiently familiar with Randy's beat to know approximately where he would be at any given time.

The worst that could happen, assuming something did break during that crucial period, would be that Randy Kennan couldn't be found. So he'd tell them that he'd taken a snooze on a side street and that the radio had broken down—he'd see that it was broken, too, before he turned in that night—and they might dock him a few days' salary or at the worst put him back to pounding a beat.

It was the best that Randy could figure out.

At ten minutes to three he got a call to go to the corner of Broadway and Sixty-ninth. Street fight.

"The sons of bitches will just have to keep on fighting," he said to himself, and then swung the patrol car south and started downtown. At Fifty-ninth Street, he turned east and headed for the Queensboro Bridge. It was a little longer than taking either the Triboro or the Midtown Tunnel, but he didn't want to pass through a tollgate. A patrol car in the heavy Saturday afternoon traffic between New York and Long Island would never be noticed. A patrol car going through a toll might.

Keeping a careful eye on his wrist watch, Randy held the car at a steady speed. He had timed the trip on a half dozen different occasions and he knew at just what point he should be at just what time. He knew that it was absolutely essential that he arrived at the track at exactly the right moment. A minute or two early wouldn't make too much difference. But as much as ten seconds late would be fatal.

He picked up the Parkway out near Forest Hills and observed that he was right on the button. He smiled, and holding the wheel with one hand, reached into his tunic for a cigarette.

At exactly four-thirty he swung into the boulevard running parallel with the race track. At four thirty-five, he turned into a narrow, asphalt paved street which ran down the side where the horses were stabled. A uniformed cop, standing in the center of the street idly directing the few cars which were leaving early, waved casually as he went by. Randy nodded his head and drove down toward the main office building which formed the rear of the clubhouse.

The sound of the crowds in the grandstands reached his ears. He knew then that the horses were off in the seventh race. The Canarsie Stakes.

There were half a dozen cars violating the no-parking ordinance on the street. A single pedestrian walked slowly away from one car as Randy drew adjacent to the clubhouse. He pulled up to the curb, alongside the high blank outside wall of the clubhouse, which abutted the street.

He looked down at his watch and saw that the minute hand was just passing the four-forty mark.

And then he heard the steady, overwhelming roar of the crowd inside the track come to a sudden, paralyzing silence. A moment later and that roar once more broke into a frenzied, hysterical cacophony.

Randy was an experienced cop. He knew the sound of a riot when he heard one.

Leaning out of the side of the car, he looked at the row of three windows, some seventy feet up on that blank concrete wall.

❃{CHAPTER VIII}❃

It was eight-thirty in the morning when Maurice Cohen reached the corner of Southern Boulevard and a Hundred and Forty-ninth Street. He went to a newsstand and bought a scratch sheet and then he found a crowded cafeteria. He ordered a cup of coffee and spread the sheet out on the table, taking a fountain pen from his inside breast pocket. He spent exactly forty-five minutes marking up the sheet. Then he carefully folded it and put it in his side coat pocket. He paid for the coffee and left.

Entering the bank on the corner near the subway steps, he strolled casually to the nearest teller's cage. He pushed a five dollar bill under the grill and asked the girl for two two-dollar rolls of nickels. She smiled and gave them to him, along with a dollar change.

Maurice dropped one roll in each side pocket.

He was armed for his afternoon's work. Maurice knew that a roll of forty nickels was just as effective as a blackjack—and there was no risk of facing a Sullivan Law charge in case he had to use it.

Riding downtown, he opened a morning tabloid and checked the train schedules in an ad on the sporting page. He decided to take the twelve-thirty, which would get him out in plenty of time to get down on the daily double. He wanted to have tickets on every race—just in case. At least it would prove, should there be a rumble and he find himself arrested, that he had a legitimate reason for going to the track in the first place.

Getting off the train at Grand Central Station, he climbed up to the street level and walked east on Forty-second Street. He went into the lobby of a tall office building between Lexington and Third Avenues and waited for an elevator. He knew the room number without looking it up on the board.

Mr. Soskin's secretary came out within a minute of the time he sent his name in. She knew him and smiled.

"Busy right now," she said. "Is there anything I can do, or would you rather wait?"

He told her he'd wait.

Fifteen minutes later she returned and beckoned him into the lawyer's private office.

Harry Soskin didn't bother to stand up. He waved a casual greeting and waited until the girl had left the room before saying anything.

Maurice sat down and for the first time lighted the cigar he'd been carrying since he got up that morning.

"Well, boy," Harry Soskin said, "what's the rumble? Don't tell me you're crapped up with the parole officer."

Maurice shook his head.

"No trouble there," he said. "I take care of him."

He smiled thinly and reached into his inside coat pocket and took out his wallet. Carefully he extracted a hundred dollar bill and tossed it across the desk to the lawyer.

"I'm going to be out on Long Island this afternoon," he said. "Queens County. I expect to be back here in town no later than six-thirty this afternoon. If I am, I want you to give me a phone number where I can reach you at that time. At exactly six-thirty. And if I shouldn't call—well, there is just a chance I might be being held by the police. In that case, I want to get sprung on bail—as soon as possible."

Soskin looked at him silently for several seconds and then slowly shook his head.

"Maurice my boy," he said. "I am the last person in the world to give advice—especially for free. But I don't think you should take any chances; not while you are still on parole."

"I'm not taking any chances," Maurice said shortly. "Anyway your advice is not free. That's a hundred bucks I just tossed you. But I didn't come for advice."

"What will the charge be—that is assuming you are not back in town by six-thirty?"

"Nothing much," Maurice said. "Possibly assault; simple assault, that is. More likely I may just happen to be picked up for questioning."

The attorney looked wise and nodded.

"You know what town?"

Maurice shook his head and laughed.

"What do you want to be, an accessory before the fact?" he asked. "No, Harry, I don't know what town. But let's say Jamaica wouldn't be too far off. Anyway, that's what I'm paying a hundred bucks for. So you could maybe find out what town. And don't forget, they got state cops, as well as county and local out that way."

Harry Soskin reached for a cigarette from the half empty pack lying on the desk. He held one in his hand but didn't light it.

"How big a bond would it be, maybe?"

Maurice shrugged.

"Who knows?"

The lawyer carefully picked up the hundred dollar bill, folded it twice and stuffed it into his breast pocket.

"O.K.," he said. "Can do. You want to leave me some money for a bond maybe?"

"Use the hundred."

"The hundred is my fee."

Maurice laughed, without humor, reached back for his wallet. He took out another hundred and handed it over.

"If that isn't enough," he said, "don't stop working. I got more. And I want it back," he added, "just in case I do make that call at six-thirty."

"Telephone me here," Soskin said. "I'll be waiting."

Maurice stood up and started for the door.

"Be seeing you," he said.

The lawyer said nothing, but merely watched him with curious eyes.

Having time to kill after he left the attorney's office, Maurice started walking across town to Penn Station. Halfway there he passed a newsreel theater. He looked at his watch and then turned and went back. He found a seat in the last row. It wasn't until the cartoon came on that he left.

He almost missed the twelve-thirty special to the track and as it was, the train being overcrowded, he had to stand up all the way out. Getting off the train, he followed the crowd to the box office. He bought a general admission and a ticket to the clubhouse. Inside the lobby of the building, he stopped and picked up a program. Then he climbed the stairs to the second floor and the main lobby leading out onto the clubhouse boxes and stands.

It took him several minutes, because of the crowd, but he found the daily double window and taking a moment to check the scratch sheet he had marked up that morning, he followed the long line to the grill. He asked for three two dollar tickets—on numbers one and six. It would, he reflected, take a god-given miracle to bring either horse in a winner, let alone both of them. He wanted those tickets after the races were over, just in case.

He was strolling past Big Mike's bar, directly opposite the door marked "PRIVATE," as the bugles blew for the first race.

He checked his wrist watch with the clock in the center of the bar, glanced only very casually at Big Mike and then kept on walking out into the stands.

At the end of the fourth race, he still had to collect his first winning bet.

At the end of the fifth race, he went to the bar and stood at one end, the far end away from the double doors leading out into the stands. He was not more than thirty feet from that door marked "PRIVATE." The door that he knew led directly into the main business offices of the race track. He ordered a bottle of beer and sipped it slowly.

At the end of the sixth race he returned to the same spot. This time he ordered Scotch and soda. Big Mike waited on him and when he received his change from a five dollar bill, Maurice pushed back a fifty-cent piece.

Big Mike looked up at him, smiled, and nodded.

"Subway," he said, under his breath, and turned and flipped the coin into an old-fashioned glass standing on the back bar.

Maurice nursed the drink until after the horses were at the post for the beginning of the seventh race—the Canarsie Stakes. He had no ticket on any horse for the classic.

He was still standing there, leaning casually against the bar, when the fight started.

* * * * *

Slowly one tiny, bloodshot eye opened and Tex looked up into the round moon face leaning down over him. The woman's heavy hand lifted again and slapped him twice, once on each side of the face.

"Say," he said. "Say, wadda hell is..."

"Get up," she said. "Goddamn it, Big Boy, get up. You said I should get you up no matter what."

She reached down then and grabbed one edge of the stained, gray sheet and with a sudden jerk, pulled it from the bed.

He lay there, huge, sprawling, stark naked. Then he opened the other eye, shook his head a couple of times and struggled to a sitting position on the side of the bed.

"For Chris' sake," he said. "Gimme a sheet or somethin'."

The blonde, her large flat face pale and dead looking, coughed and then laughed.

"You look good, big boy, the way you are," she said. But she picked up the sheet and tossed it back to him. "I better get you a pick-me-up."

Tex stared at her for a minute and then looked toward the drawn green curtain, fighting to keep the sunlight out of the room.

"Where the hell am I?" he asked, his voice thick.

"You're in Hoboken, brother," the blonde said. "In the finest damn whore house in the State of New Jersey." She reached for the half empty whiskey bottle sitting beside the large washbasin on the old-fashioned maple bureau. She began to pour a long drink in a dirty jelly glass. Tex took his eyes from her and started to look around the room. For the first time he saw the redhead who lay next to him on the inside of the double bed.

"Who the hell is she?" he said. "Fur Chris' sake, who..."

"She's your girl, you dumb bastard," the blonde said.

"Well, who are you then?" Tex asked, automatically reaching out for the drink she was handing him.

"I'm your girl, too, Big Boy," the blonde said, and laughed. "Hell, don't you remember? You come in here last night, half stiff already and you said you wanted to have one hell of a time. Don't you remember? Said you'd be in jail in another twenty-four hours and you wanted to get fixed up right for a long stay."

"Aw, for..."

"So you drank two bottles a booze and then Flo and I..."

Tex wasn't listening. He had lifted the glass and drained it in one gulp. Suddenly he was bending over gagging.

It took an hour and two pots of coffee to get him on his feet, dressed and ready to leave. By that time he was reasonably sober. The redhead was still sleeping as he said goodbye to the blonde.

"You come back—any time," she said. "But you better go now. You was saying all night about some job out at the race track..."

"Forget what I said," Tex told her, suddenly short and abrupt. "Forget what I said."

He opened the door and started down the hallway.

"Good-by now," she called after him.

When he got out of the Hudson tubes on the Manhattan side, his head was splitting and he was tempted to stop in at the nearest tavern and have a quick one. But then he shook his head and walked over to the taxi parked in front of the kiosk.

Climbing in the back, he said, "Penn Station, Mac. An' what train will I be making for the track?"

The driver pushed the car into gear and then spoke without turning his head.

"The twelve-thirty," he said. "That is if I can get through this god damned traffic at all today."

Getting off the train at the race track, Tex turned and started in the opposite direction from the clubhouse. It took him three blocks before he came to the restaurant. He went in and found a stool at the bar. A tired-looking, middle-aged waitress asked what he wanted.

"About a half a gallon of orange juice," he said.

"You want a small or a large?"

"Large," he said. "An' gimme an order of ham and eggs."

"We got no..."

"Gimme a double order of eggs," he said. "You got eggs, ain't yuh. I want four eggs, sunny side up. An' a double order of toast and a couple a cups a coffee."

The woman looked at him wildly for a minute and then wordlessly turned and started for the kitchen. She came back a few minutes later with a small orange juice and an order of bacon and eggs and toast. Two eggs. He had to remind her about the coffee.

Walking back toward the track, he began to feel all right again. He was walking slowly and half daydreaming, remembering the blonde and trying to remember the redhead, when the sound of a roar from the crowd in the stands came to him. He stopped, looked up suddenly, and then hurried on. The horses were lining up for the second race when he paid his entrance fee.

It took him until the beginning of the third race to find the bar in back of which Big Mike was mixing drinks. He went to the bar and stood at the end served by one of the other barkeeps. The crowd was already leaving to go out to the track.

"What will it be, sir?"

Tex looked up at the white aproned bartender and frowned.

He thought for a moment, rubbing one dirty nailed finger down the side of his unshaven chin.

"A shot a whiskey, some hot sauce an' an ice cube. In a beer glass," he added.

For a moment the bartender looked perplexed. "You mean a shot of Worcestershire in the whiskey. Right? Rye or bourbon?"

"That's right," Tex said. "Hot sauce. Any kind a whiskey is O.K."

He nursed the drink during the running of the third race.

When the horses came out for the fourth race, Tex went out to the stands. He stayed there for the running of that race as well as the fifth race. He neither bet nor showed the slightest interest in the tote board. After the prices had been posted on the fifth race, he once more returned to the clubhouse lobby. He went back to the bar, this time crowding himself into a spot directly in front of Big Mike. He waited patiently for several minutes while Mike served half a dozen other patrons.

It wasn't until almost the start of the sixth race that Big Mike asked him what he wanted.

"Service, you Irish slob," Tex said in a low voice.

Big Mike stared at him for several seconds.

"And what would yours be?" he said then.

"Bottle a beer," Tex said.

He stood and drank slowly, stretching the bottle out until the end of the race. Then, before the crowd began to come in from the stands, he ordered another bottle of beer. It was five minutes after four, according to the clock over the bar.

At twenty-five minutes past four the bugle blew calling the horses out to the post for the Canarsie Stakes. The big race would be off within another twelve minutes.

Already people were beginning to drift away from the bar. Big Mike had found time to rest for a second between pouring drinks, and he was standing in front of Tex, mopping up the wet mahogany with a bar rag.

Tex looked directly at him and spoke in a loud voice.

"You son of a bitch," he said, "whadda yu mean taking my drink before I finished with it?"

Out of the corner of his eye he noticed two or three men who had started to leave the bar, turn and hesitate.

"I beg your pardon, sir," Mike said. "I..."

"Don't tell me you didn't take it, yu bastard," Tex said. By this time he had raised his voice to a yell.

A dozen persons, starting through the gate into the stands, hesitated and turned back toward the bar. Almost at once a block began to form at the double doors.

Tex hesitated a moment and then reached down with one hand and picked up his beer glass.

He lifted it high and smashed it down on the bar and the glass shattered and splintered into a thousand pieces.

"You stole my drink, yu Irish bastard," he screamed. "Now get me another before I knock your god damned..."

As he yelled the words he was aware of the crowd rapidly forming around him. He also saw, out of the corner of his eye, a large, broad-shouldered man quickly edging his way through the crowd from over by the cashier's windows. Tex estimated it would take the man about a half minute to reach him.

He leaned as far as he could across the bar and with his open hand slapped Big Mike across the face.

Big Mike let out a roar and putting one hand on the edge of the mahogany, he stepped up on the stainless steel sink under the bar and quickly vaulted across.

He landed like a cat, directly in front of Tex.

Tex started yelling again and his hand shot out and he slapped Big Mike again.

By this time the place was in an uproar. The other bartenders were rushing down toward them and the cashier was blowing a small whistle. The big man Tex had spotted coming through the crowd had not yet reached him. The door into the grandstands was completely blocked and not one out of a hundred in the crowd really knew what was taking place.

Even as Tex pushed Big Mike away from himself, his eye

went to the clock. They'd be off in the Canarsie Stakes within the next three minutes.

Big Mike had his arm in a steel-like grip as the Pinkerton man reached Tex's side. Tex tore his arm free and his fist shot out and caught the broad-shouldered man squarely between the eyes.

The Pinkerton man had his blackjack out as Tex saw the door marked "PRIVATE" open quickly. It closed a second later behind another large, well-built man who had cop written all over him.

Tex saw the blackjack descending and he shifted so that he caught the blow on his shoulder. He slugged the private cop a second time and this time he gave it everything he had. The man fell to the floor like a log, as half a dozen onlookers struggled to get out of his way.

Tex felt the thud of the billy on the back of his head.

It didn't knock him out, but he started to slump to his knees.

He felt hands grab each of his arms.

As two detectives started to propel him toward a door marked EXIT, which he guessed led to the staircase, he saw Mike helping the first Pinkerton man to his feet.

He also heard a terrific wave of sound from the direction of the grandstand. He smiled. He felt fine. Johnny would be pleased.

They were off in the big race of the day. The Canarsie Stakes.

* * * * *

Nikki left Catskill, New York, on the Greyhound bus at midnight, Friday. He carried the 30-06 Winchester with the telescopic sight, broken down in three parts—stock, barrel and sight—carefully wrapped in rags. He had put it in an empty trombone case which he had picked up several days before in a hock shop down on Third Avenue.

The gun came from Abercrombie and Fitch's and it had cost

turn two hundred and ten dollars.

After three days' practice up at the lodge, in the hills back of Kingston, he had grown attached to the gun. He hoped that it might just barely be possible to hang on to it after it had done its work. He had sighted it in perfectly and he had been especially pleased to discover that the use of the silencer barely interfered with his aim.

The bus arrived in New York around three-thirty and Nikki went at once to a small midtown hotel. He checked in and left word to be called at eight o'clock.

He was already dressed and shaved and ready to check out when the phone rang and the desk clerk told him it was 8 a.m. He had slept badly and he was tense and high-strung. He began to chain smoke almost at once.

This is the way he wanted to be; he liked to be on edge when he had a job to do.

After a quick breakfast, Nikki went to the garage on upper Broadway which advertised rental cars—the one which specialized in convertibles and foreign sports jobs.

He showed them a Florida driver's license and false identification papers and then left a hundred dollar deposit on an MG. The phony papers had cost him fifty dollars and he had paid another twenty for a stolen Florida plate. Nikki had contacts where almost anything could be bought for a price.

Before he took the car out, he checked to see that it had canvas side curtains.

They filled the tank with gas and he put the trombone case behind the front seat and then drove south on Broadway. He made only one stop before taking the East Side drive up to the Triboro Bridge. He pulled up in front of an Army and Navy surplus store and went in and bought a gray army blanket.

He had a cup of coffee in Jamaica.

It took him more than an hour to find a secluded spot at the end of a dirt road out near Freeport. He pulled into the shade of a clump of bushes and got out of the car. The pliers and screw driver were wrapped up in a small package with the Florida license tag. In less than ten minutes he had the New York plate off the car and had substituted the other one. Later, he found a sea food place in Freeport and had a good lunch.

He was back, cruising slowly about a mile from the track, at twelve-thirty. At twelve-forty he followed the route Johnny had marked on the map and which he had memorized and drove up to the northeast parking lot. The MG's top was up, but he had not used the side curtains. The army blanket was spread over his legs and covered his lap and his feet, where they rested on the pedals.

The man at the entrance to the lot yelled at him as he drove across the double lane to the gate.

"Use one of the other lots, buddy," the attendant told him as he pulled up to a stop. "This one ain't open yet."

Nikki looked up at the man, his eyes half closed behind the dark glasses.

"Listen, Mac," he said. "I'm a paraplegic. I wanted to get in this lot and watch the races from my car."

He took out his wallet as he spoke and reached in, taking hold of a ten dollar bill.

"Say, they can get you a chair..."

"1 know," Nikki said, "but I just can't manage it. Particularly in the crowds. And I have to leave before the races are over."

The man hesitated for a second and Nikki held out the ten.

The attendant looked down and saw the blanket.

"Oh the hell with it," he said. "Go ahead on in. We ain't open yet so you can skip..."

"Take it and get yourself a lucky bet," Nikki said.

The man hesitated, then, almost shyly, reached for the bill.

"Go on in," he said gruffly and lifted the chain barring the entrance way.

Nikki maneuvered the car into the southeast corner of the parking lot and pulled up seven feet away from the low rail fence marking its boundary. The space was next to the long aisle leading to the exit and in such a position as to make it possible to pull out either by going forward or by turning to the left.

There was nothing on that side but a second aisle; there was one place for a car to park behind him and one for a car to park to his right.

He sat back and lighted a fresh cigarette.

They started running cars into the lot ten minutes before the first race was due to begin.

Nikki was reaching back for the trombone case when the man came alongside the MG and leaned on the door. It was the lot attendant who had taken his ten dollar bill.

"Bought you a program, chum," the man said.

Nikki looked up, startled, and then quickly smiled.

"Thanks."

"And if you want anything else, I can get it for you."

Nikki thanked him again.

"Not a thing," he said. "I already got a couple of bets down with a bookie at my hotel."

By two-thirty the lot was filled. A Packard limousine, chauffeur driven, had parked next to the MG and its four passengers had gone to the clubhouse. The chauffeur waited only a few moments and then followed them in the direction of the box office. Behind the MG was a Caddie convertible. A man and a girl had parked it and had left at once.

From where Nikki sat behind the wheel he had a perfect view of the curve of the track where the horses broke at the three quarter pole for the home stretch. The track was approximately two hundred yards away and there was nothing between the car and the track but green turf.

At the end of the fifth race, Nikki found the side curtains and put them up. There was a small oblong of plastic glass in each one. Then he reached forward and opened the hasps on the windshield. He had to loosen the top in order to drop the windshield so that it lay flat and parallel with the hood of the car.

He waited until five minutes before the start of the seventh race before taking the rifle from the trombone case. It was tricky, doing it under the blanket, but he had assembled and reassembled it so many times within the last few days that he had little difficulty.

He attached the silencer and threw a shell into the firing chamber. There were five shells in the clip, but he didn't believe he'd have to use more than one. He didn't think he'd have time to use more than two at the most.

It was a mile and a quarter race and the horses had to pass the grandstand twice.

Nikki, completely oblivious to the roar of the crowd, held a pair of field glasses to his eyes. He was watching the colors—brown and silver.

Black Lightning was away to a slow start, but he picked up on the backstretch and as they came past the grandstands for the first time he took the lead.

The horses were bunched the second time around the backstretch, with Black Lightning in front by a full length.

Nikki didn't bother to look around to see if he was being observed. It wouldn't matter now. He was going to do it anyway.

He pulled the blanket away and lifted the rifle, poking the long barrel through the open windshield.

He took his time and waited until Black Lightning was directly opposite. Then, carefully leading the target as though he were aiming at a fast moving buck, he drew a bead.

The sound of the shot, muffled as it was by the silencer, was completely lost in the steady, rhythmic roar of sixty thousand voices as the crowd urged its favorites on.

Nikki waited just long enough to see the horses behind Black Lightning begin to pile up when the favorite stumbled and fell.

There was no one on duty at the gate, a minute later, as Nikki wheeled the MG through the exit.

* * * * *

Val Cannon said, "You're not talking."

He leaned back, his hands supporting him on the desk and his back to it. He looked at the girl sitting in the chair two feet away, facing him.

Sherry Peatty looked up at him, her eyes glassy with fear. She started to say something and at once her mouth filled with blood. She leaned forward to spit it out and then she began to vomit.

Val watched her, hooded eyes cool, almost amused.

"You know something," he said, "so why not tell me? What do you want to do this to yourself for?"

He waited until she looked up again. She started to weave and would have fallen if the fat man standing behind her chair hadn't reached over and held her up by her arms.

"It's four-thirty," Val said. "I got all the time in the world. Right now I'm going out and get a drink. When I come back, I want you to tell me what you know."

He turned to the desk and picked up his leather belt and casually threaded it around the waistband of his trousers. He watched Sherry where she sat, half conscious in the chair, naked down to her hips.

"You got cagey with the wrong guy," he said. "Think it over. Tell me when they're doing it. Tell me everything you know. I'll be back in a few minutes and God help you if you're still stubborn."

Sherry opened her split lips. She tried to say something and then she began to cough. A second later and she slumped.

"Fainted," the fat man said, shrugging.

❊{CHAPTER IX}❊

Four years he had been waiting for it. Waiting for this day, this Saturday in the last week of July.

There hadn't been a single day, not one of the three hundred and sixty-five days in each of those long, heartbreaking years, that he hadn't at some time or other thought of how he would be feeling at this exact moment. The moment that he would be waking up in a strange bed in a third-rate hotel, broke, in debt, a parole violator. And knowing that before sunset he'd be either dead or he'd have found the money which would bring him the escape he had always been seeking. The escape which, for him, only money could buy.

It was the first thing that came to his mind as he opened his eyes.

He reached over and took the pack of cigarettes from the night table. He knocked one out and then fumbled around until he found the lighter. Laying back on the pillow, he inhaled deeply; slowly letting the smoke escape from between thin, well-denned lips.

He felt great.

He took another puff, and he spoke in a clear, low voice, directing his words at the dirt-encrusted ceiling.

"Brother, this is it!"

He laughed then, realizing that he was talking to himself. Turning his head, he was able to see the face of his wrist watch where it lay on the night table beside the pack of cigarettes. It was exactly eight o'clock.

He had plenty of time.

The telephone was over on the scarred writing desk next to the door leading into the bathroom. He got up, completely naked, and went over to the chair in front of the desk. The curtains covering the single, opened window were pulled apart and he could look directly into a room across the court. The window was closed and too dirty to see much through. He knew, however, that he himself could be seen. He laughed again. It didn't bother him in the slightest. Today, nothing bothered him.

The clerk at the desk in the lobby told him over the phone that they didn't have room service. "Hell, we ain't even got a restaurant," the voice said. "I can send up a bottle and some ice and soda, though, with a bellhop," he added.

"Too early," Johnny said, "but you tell that bellboy to go out and get me a container of coffee, some orange juice and a couple of hard rolls and it's worth a fast buck to him."

"Will do," the clerk said.

There was no shower in the old-fashioned bathroom so Johnny ran a tub full of water. He waited, however, until his breakfast showed up, before climbing in.

The bellhop brought a paper along and Johnny casually glanced at the headlines as he ate. He sat by the open window, stripped down to his shorts. His mind, however, was not on the news. He was carefully going over everything which he had done during the last couple of days since he had left Marvin Unger's apartment to take the hotel room. He wanted to be absolutely sure he hadn't overlooked anything.

It had been a smart move, checking into the hotel. He had found himself growing jittery, hanging around Unger. Another day of it and something would have had to give. The tension was too much. For a while he had considered staying at the room up on a Hundred and Third Street, but then he had decided against that. He wanted to keep that place for one purpose and one purpose only.

He smiled to himself as he thought of Joe Piano. Joe hadn't

liked the idea when Johnny had told him that Randy was going to stop by. Joe couldn't understand what he was doing playing around with a cop. It had taken a little explaining. At least there was one thing about Joe; he hadn't shown any unhealthy curiosity.

Johnny had stopped by to pick up the suitcase which held the sub-machine gun. Joe, answering the doorbell, had asked him into the kitchen; wanted him to have a glass of wine. It had happened on Friday afternoon. Then they had gone up to Johnny's room.

"Taking this out now," Johnny told him, indicating the suitcase. "Tomorrow afternoon a friend of mine is stopping by. He'll leave a bundle for me. He's a cop."

"A cop?"

"Yeah, drives a prowl car."

"Funny kind of a friend to have," Joe said.

"He's O.K. A very special cop." Johnny winked at him. "He's leaving this bundle for me sometime around six or six-thirty at the latest. I'll be in early in the evening to pick it up. And that's the last you'll see of me."

Joe nodded, noncommittal.

Johnny took a folded bill out of his watch pocket. It was a fifty.

"I'd like to see that Patsy gets this," he said.

"That isn't necessary," Joe told him. "I can take care of Patsy all right."

"I know," Johnny said. "But he's a good friend of mine."

Joe said nothing but he did reach out and take the bill. Johnny left soon afterward.

"The idea of that cop leaves me cold," Joe told him as he walked down the long hallway to open the gate for him, "but any friend of the boy's has got to be all right."

Johnny found a cab on Second Avenue and told the driver to take him to Penn Station. He carried the suitcase into the lobby and found the bank of steel lockers. Checking the suitcase, he took the key and put it in an envelope. That night he had a messenger service drop it off at Big Mike's apartment.

Buying the brief case had been easy. He got the kind you carry under your arm and that you close with a zipper. The duffel bag had been harder to find. He finally dug one up in a chain sporting goods and auto accessory store. It was made of heavy canvas, leather reinforced and had a drawstring at the open end. Folded flat, it just fitted into the brief case.

When he had called Fay around nine o'clock at her home, she had quickly memorized the number he gave her and then had gone out to a pay booth and called him back. She'd wanted to see him, but he had told her it would be better if they didn't meet.

"It'll only be another twenty-four hours," he'd said. "Then it's the rest of our lives, kid."

She told him that everything was ready. He detected the slight quiver in her voice and he hung up as quickly as possible. He knew that she'd be better off not seeing him; not even talking with him.

And then he'd gone back to the hotel. There was nothing else to do. Getting to sleep had been a problem. He knew it would be and he'd considered taking sleeping pills, or perhaps a half bottle of whiskey. But he'd decided against either escape. He wanted to be sure to be in top form the next morning. He didn't want a hang-over or even as much as the trace of one. He didn't want the dopey feeling that the sleeping pills would be sure to leave.

The lack of sleep itself wouldn't bother him. It would, in fact, merely keep him keyed up and tense. That he wanted.

But he had slept. In spite of everything he awakened in the morning feeling completely relaxed and completely rested.

Now, as he slowly ate his breakfast, he tried not to think of anything but the immediate moment. Everything was set in his mind, his plans were made down to the finest detail. He didn't want to think about what might happen during the crucial hour this Saturday afternoon. Thinking about it wouldn't help. He'd already done his thinking.

Johnny Clay left the hotel at eleven o'clock. He checked out, carrying the leather suitcase he had used at Unger's in one hand, the brief case in the other. The suitcase held the new clothes he'd bought during the last two days. The old stuff he left upstairs. He was wearing the slacks and the checkered sports coat he would wear that afternoon at the track.

It was a warm day and he was tempted to remove the coat, but then decided against it. Under the coat he had two shirts; one a soft tan with an open collar, over that a deep blue shirt, the collar closed. He wore neutral tan, low shoes, tan socks and a soft gray felt hat with a wide brim, turned down in the front. In his coat pocket was a second rolled-up, light-weight felt hat, powder blue with a low crown and a narrow brim.

The glasses had dark green lens. His first move after leaving the hotel was finding a cab. He ordered the driver to take him to La Guardia Airport.

He checked the suitcase at the airport and then went to the restaurant and ordered coffee and toast. He spread the early edition of the World Telegram on the table and turned to the sporting pages.

At one o'clock Johnny left the airport in another cab. He was carrying the brief case under his arm.

He arrived at the race track at one-forty.

The cab driver had been willing to go along with him. Johnny told him he'd give him ten bucks for the cab and pay his entrance fee into the grandstand. And he wanted to be taken back to New York after the races.

"The only thing is," Johnny said, "I got to leave the second the seventh race is over. Have an appointment back in town and I won't have any time to spare. I'll plan to be out at the parking lot by the time the race ends. I won't wait for the results. I want you to be there and ready to leave."

It was O.K. with the cabbie.

"Hell," he said. "I'm getting paid, I'll be there. Anyway, I don't bet 'em; I just like to see them run."

They'd found a parking space in the lot at the south end of

the track. The cab was one of the last cars in the lot, which would make it easy for them to get out. Johnny got out of the back, slamming the door. He reached through the window and handed the driver a ten dollar bill.

"Buy your ticket out of that," he said, "and use the change to try your luck. You be here waiting when I get here and you get another ten when we pull into New York."

"I'll be here."

Johnny turned toward the clubhouse. The brief case was under his arm. He walked slowly. He had plenty of time.

* * * * *

It was as he knew it would be. He never yet had gone to a track without that feeling. That strange, subtle sense of excitement. Even as he stood at the box office buying his ticket, he became infected by it. There was something about the track that always gave it to him.

The first race was already over and done with and the crowd, for the moment, was quiet. But he caught the inevitable undercurrent of excitement.

Walking through the downstairs lobby and stopping off to buy his program, he found himself unconsciously fingering the loose folded bills in his pants pocket. He laughed quietly to himself. Here he was, on the threshold of a caper which would mean more than a million dollars, and he couldn't wait to get the program open and place a bet on the second race.

Walking up the stairs, he went through the main lobby and passed within thirty feet of the bar behind which Big Mike was rushing drinks to an impatient clientele. Out of the corner of his eye he spotted the door marked "Private." The one leading into the main business offices and the one out of which he knew he would be coming before that afternoon would be over and done with.

He also quickly looked in the direction of the other door. The door which was set flush into the wall and through which he would have to pass in order to get into the employees' locker

room. The door which would have to be surreptitiously opened
from the inside to permit his entrance.

He was aware of Big Mike moving behind the bar. There was
no sign of Maurice and no sign of Tex.

He went out into the stands, out into the hot yellow sunlight.
He had to shoulder his way through the crowd at the door.
He found a seat well up in the stands and slouching into it, he
dropped the brief case between his feet on the concrete floor.
He opened the program and looked over the horses in the sec-
ond race. Then he looked up and checked the morning line.

When the horses reached the post for the second race, Johnny stood up. He took off his hat and left it and his program on
the seat. Then he made his way back into the clubhouse. He
went to the ten dollar window and put down a win bet on the
number three horse. The tote board had it at eight to five.

Johnny didn't want to start the day depending on long shots
to come in.

The number three horse won by three and a half lengths.

Returning to his seat after he collected his winnings, he
glanced at the clock as he passed Big Mike's bar. His wrist
watch was less than a minute slow.

He was back again at the buyer's windows long before the
fifth race started. This time he did what Unger had done several
days before. There were a half dozen ten dollar windows and he
went to each of them in turn. By the time he ended up he had
a ticket on every horse in the race.

When he got back to his seat, just before the horses left the
post, he found a large, red-faced woman sitting in it. She was
holding his hat and program.

He stood in front of her for a moment, undecided. She
looked up at him and grinned.

"Just had to sit down for a second," she said breathing heavily. "I'm exhausted."

She started to stand up and he smiled at her.

"Stay where you are," he said. "I'll stand for this one."

She began to protest, but he insisted. She had handed him

his hat and program, looking grateful.

He walked down through the stands to the rail as the horses were running. When the sixth horse came in, he didn't have to search through the tickets to find the right one. He had put them in order.

He was about tenth in line at the window—George Peatty's window.

Johnny held his thumb on the ticket as he pushed it through the grill. He was watching George's face.

Peatty's face was yellow and his mouth was trembling even before he looked up. And then, a moment later, as he reached for the ticket, he lifted his eyes and stared directly at Johnny. He nodded, almost imperceptibly. He counted out the money and pushed it through the grill work.

At four-twenty, Johnny was leaning against the wall some five feet from the door leading into the locker rooms. He had the scratch sheet in his hand and was resting it on the brief case. He held a pencil in his other hand and was making casual marks on the sheet. But his eyes were not seeing what his hands were doing.

His hat brim was pulled well forward and the dark glasses concealed his eyes.

Johnny was watching the end of the bar where Tex stood.

He didn't move when the fight started.

Once he had to step aside as a large man pushed past him. But he still didn't make his move. Didn't make it until he saw the door of the private office open.

It was while they were rushing Tex toward the exit stairway that Johnny sidled over to the entrance to the locker room. Every eye in the lobby was on Tex and the detectives surrounding him when Johnny felt the door move behind him. A second later and he turned and quickly slipped into the employees' locker room.

George, pale and his hands shaking, quickly closed the door behind him. He looked for a moment at Johnny, saying not a word. Then he turned and a moment later had disappeared in the direction of the exit leading out behind the cashiers' cages.

A quick glance around the room showed Johnny that there was no one in it, unless they were in one of the line of toilet stalls. Johnny didn't have to look at the diagram he had in his pocket. He knew exactly where Big Mike's locker was. The duplicate key was in his hand.

It took him less than half a minute to open the locker and take out the flower box. A moment later and he had slipped into one of the toilets and had closed and latched the door.

He was assembling the gun and inserting a clip of shells as the horses left the post for the start of the Canarsie Stakes.

Johnny had opened the brief case and was taking out the duffel bag when he heard the door slam.

Two men entered the room and they were standing not ten feet away. From their conversation, Johnny knew at once that they were cashiers, taking a breather while the race was being run.

"What the hell was that fracas out there?" one voice said.

"Just some drunken bum giving one of the bartenders a hard time. Christ, did you see Frank leap into it with that blackjack!"

"It's time one of those god damned Pinkertons earned his dough," the first man said.

Johnny smiled grimly.

They'd be earning their dough in another three minutes, he said to himself. And if these guys didn't get out before then, they'd be earning theirs, too.

Even as the thought crossed his mind, the two men began to move away. Johnny's hand reached for the latch.

* * * * *

Maxie Flam couldn't have weighed a hundred and ten pounds dripping wet. But in order to keep his weight down, now, at thirty-six, he not only had to starve himself, he had to take the pills and he had to really work out.

He was thinking, as the horses came up to the starting line, that thank God, he only had another season to go. Then he'd retire. He'd be through with the tortuous routine once and for all. And he was doing something that damn few jockeys had ever been able to do. He was retiring on the money he had saved since the day he had ridden his first mount back when he was in knee pants.

Maxie had played it smart. He'd never bet on a horse in his life. Even today, with Black Lightning's broad back between his spindly legs, he hadn't bet. He knew Black Lightning was going to win. Knew it just as sure as he knew his name.

Almost unconsciously his eyes went up to where Mrs. Galway Dicks sat in the box with her two daughters and the men who had accompanied them to the track.

Mrs. Dicks had been upset as she always was. It annoyed her when Maxie wouldn't put a bet on the horse he was riding. She had wanted to get someone else, but the trainer had insisted on Maxie. The trainer was smarter than Mrs. Dicks would ever be.

"But I can't understand, Maxie," she had said. "You say we've got to win. So why don't you put something down on the horse yourself?"

Maxie hadn't bothered to explain.

"I never bet," he'd said, and let it go at that.

There may have been better jockeys—although in complete and unassuming fairness, Maxie told himself that there hadn't been a great many of them. But even the greats, Sande and the rest of them, had ended up broke. They may have booted in more winners, but they'd still ended up broke. Not Maxie. He didn't have to be the greatest, but by God, he was one of the smartest.

At the end of this season he'd have a quarter of a million in annuities. And then he was going to quit. He'd go down to his breeding farm in Maryland and he'd never see another race track as long as he'd live. And the only thing he'd ever ride again would be the front seat of a Cadillac convertible.

Maxie was smart.

Black Lightning reared up as a horse moved in next to him and Maxie instinctively pulled slightly on the rein and his mount danced sideways. Maxie spoke softly and soothingly under his breath.

And then they were off.

Maxie didn't rush it. He knew he had this race in the bag, but there was no reason to rush. He knew what Black Lightning could do. Not only that, but he also knew approximately what every other horse in the race could do.

Passing the grandstands on his first time around the track, Maxie kept his eyes straight ahead.

He was conscious of the crowds; he even heard, dimly in the background of his mind, the roar from the packed stands. He was aware of the color and the tension and the high excitement. But it all left him cold. He'd been in the saddle too many years to any longer feel the vicarious thrill. He was a cold, aloof, precision machine. A part of the horse itself. He was at the track for one reason and one reason only. To win the race. Nothing, nothing else at all interfered with that thought.

Going into the backstretch on the second time around, Maxie knew exactly where he stood in relationship to the other horses in the race. He spoke, in a low soft voice, almost directly into the horse's ear from where he leaned far over Black Lightning's neck. His crop just barely brushed the sweat soaked flanks of the animal.

He began to move out ahead.

It was like it always was when he had the right horse under him. He was in. He knew it.

He went into the far corner and he lengthened the gap between himself and the others by a half a length. And then he was starting around the three quarter mark and getting set for the stretch. He had decided he would spread the gap by about a length and a half. He was sure, dead sure. But he'd take no chances. It was always possible one of those others would open up.

His eyes were straight in front, on the dusty track about twenty yards ahead of Black Lightning's nose.

He never knew what happened. One second and he was sitting there, almost as though he were posting a horse in a Garden Show. Knowing, never doubting for a second that in another few seconds he would hear the old familiar roar which would let him know he was coming in in front.

And then it happened.

Later on, when Mrs. Dicks saw him in the hospital and Leo, her trainer, stood beside her and they asked him about it, he was still unable to say exactly what it was.

He only remembered that everything had been fine there, for that moment.

And then, before he knew it, Black Lightning had gone to his knees and Maxie himself was flying through the air. Hitting the track spread-eagled, he was instantly knocked unconscious.

He never heard the hysterical, agonized screams of the other horses as they piled into Black Lightning. He didn't hear the crack of breaking bones, didn't see the blood which quickly splashed and then soaked into the soft dirt of the track.

He didn't hear the wailing sirens of the ambulances as they raced across the infield.

He was completely unconscious of the sudden, horrified hush of that vast crowd in the stands. A hush which in the very intensity of its suddenness was more dramatic and perhaps even more terrible than would have been the wildest and most fanatic screaming and shouting.

The leaden slug from the 30-06 didn't kill Black Lightning. It took him just below the right eye and tore into the cheek until it struck bone and then plowed upward and came out through the back of the skull leaving a huge, four inch wide gap.

The hoof of the number three horse, crashing into that bloody gash, tore Black Lightning's brains out through the side of his head.

Alice McAndrews looked up from the typewriter. Her soft, sensuous mouth opened wide and her large blue eyes, upon which she had more than once been complimented, began to pop. She started to scream.

Holding the stock of the sub-machine gun under his right arm pit, Johnny Clay tightened his left hand on the neck of the crunched up duffel bag. He whipped it out and caught the girl across the face with it before the sound reached her lips.

And then he stepped back a pace and faced the four people in the room. His voice was just barely audible.

"One sound," he said, "one sound from any of you and I start shooting!"

The two men counting the money on the top of the wide table froze. Their hands were still in front of them, half buried in green bills. The other one, the one with the forty-five strapped to the holster at his hip, stood at the water cooler, and didn't move.

Alice McAndrews began to cry and then quickly swallowed. A second later and she slumped to the floor in a dead faint.

One of the men at the table began to move toward her.

"Leave her," Johnny said.

"You!"

He pointed his gun at the man nearest him, one of those at the table. "Take that duffel bag and start filling it. And you," he looked at the other man, "go over and take that gun out of the holster. Be awfully careful how you do it. Take it out and lay it down on the floor. Then I want the two of you to turn around and face the wall."

Johnny tossed the canvas sack onto the table.

It took less than two minutes to stuff the money in the bag. By that time the girl had begun to moan and move slightly. Johnny ignored her. He edged around until his back was to the door which led out into the stands. He had already snapped the lock on the door through which he had entered the room—the one from the employees' locker room.

"Brother, you'll..."

Johnny looked up quickly. It was the man who had had the gun strapped to his waist.

"Shut up," Johnny said. "Shut up! I'd like to kill a cop. Particularly a private cop."

He had to speak very clearly. The handkerchief over the lower part of his face made the words seem muffled even then.

He waited until the man at the table was through.

"Now," he said, indicating the safe in the corner whose door hung half open, "get the rest of it."

Through the closed door he heard the almost hysterical screaming and yelling of the crowds in the stands. He knew. He knew just what was happening out there.

It took another three minutes to get the money from the safe into the duffel bag. The bag itself was overflowing and there was still more money in the safe.

"That's all," Johnny said. "Pull the drawstring on the bag."

The man, his hands shaking so badly he had difficulty managing it, did as he was directed. Then he dropped the bag to the floor.

"Pick her up," Johnny said, motioning toward the girl. No one moved for a moment.

"You," said Johnny, looking at the private guard.

The man reached down then and lifted the girl to her feet.

The next minute would be the one which would decide.

Johnny's eyes moved quickly to the door leading from the office into the room next to it. The room which he knew held the large track staff and in which the real work was done. In that room would be some three dozen persons.

"I'm going to count three," he said, "and then I want you to open that door. You are to go through it. When you get through,"—he stopped and looked for a second at the cop who was holding the girl—"and drag her with you," he interrupted himself. "When you get through, just keep moving. I'm going to start firing through that door exactly fifteen seconds after you close it behind you. Now, before I begin counting, hand me that bag."

The man who had stuffed the bag with the money lifted it and carried it across the room to where Johnny stood. He had moved over toward the single window of the room so that he commanded all three doors. The window was wide open and he felt the slight breeze at his back.

The man dropped the duffel bag at his feet and turned and walked toward the others.

Johnny started counting.

For a split second, as the door opened and the three men and the girl pushed through it, Johnny saw a couple of startled faces in the other room, looking out at him.

He waited only until the door was closed and then he reached down with his left hand and grabbed the bag. It was too heavy and he had to drop the gun.

A moment later, never looking, he heaved the duffel bag through the window.

He didn't bother to pick up the machine gun again.

Even before he had reached the door leading out into the lobby, he had stripped the gloves from his hands. He was tearing the handkerchief from his face as he opened the door.

The whole thing had taken less than five minutes.

Johnny's right arm was out of the sleeve of the sports coat and it was half off as he slammed the door marked "PRIVATE" behind himself. He was aware of Maurice standing next to him as he dropped the sports jacket to the floor and pulled the soft felt hat from his head. He heard the shouts then. He saw the man rushing toward them.

He was only dimly conscious of the sound of flesh against flesh as Maurice's fist smashed into the man's face at his side.

And then he was pushing through the crush of bodies.

A woman's high piercing scream kept coming through the din of the crowd as Johnny shoved his way through the jammed lower lobby of the clubhouse. There were no attendants in sight as he left by the main entrance.

The sound of the sirens from the ambulances on the infield was suddenly interrupted by the shrieking of other sirens coming from outside of the track itself.

Johnny realized that the riot call had been sent in.

He found the cab driver starting to leave his seat in the taxi.

"My God," the man said, looking at him with startled eyes, "what in the hell's going on. Sounds like..."

"The hell with it," Johnny said. "Fight started at the end of the seventh. I don't know what it is, but this place is going to be a madhouse in about another three minutes. I got to get into town. Let's go."

The driver hesitated a second, then settled back behind the wheel.

"Guess you're right," he said. "We get trapped in here and we'll never get away."

Turning into the boulevard a couple of minutes later, the cabbie pulled well over to the curb and slowed up as a speeding riot car passed them.

The police officer who had been directing traffic at the intersection was no longer guarding his post.

Johnny dismissed the cab at the subway station in Long Island City.

"In a hurry," he said. "I'll make better time on the subway." He handed the man the second ten dollars.

As he started up the stairs, he was aware of the driver leaving the parked cab and heading for an adjacent tavern. The man probably wanted to hear what might be coming over the radio about the riot out at the track.

Getting off at Grand Central Station, Johnny went upstairs and ducked into the newsreel theater. He had a couple of hours to kill.

He was suddenly beginning to feel faint. He wanted to sit down.

❉{CHAPTER X}❉

In spite of the questioning, the confusion and the general all around hysteria, Big Mike was the first one to arrive at the apartment on East Thirty-first Street. He got out of the elevator and knocked on the door at exactly eight thirty-five.

Marvin Unger's face was like chalk. His voice, coming through the thin panel, sounded hoarse and frightened when he asked who it was. His hands were shaking uncontrollably as he pushed the door open from the inside.

Big Mike slipped in without a word.

The Venetian blinds were down and there was no light on, although it was past dusk.

Big Mike went to the couch and slumped.

Unger stood with his back to the door.

"Christ," he said. "Oh, Jesus Christ, I never thought it was going to be like that!"

Big Mike looked at him without expression.

"Like what?" he said.

"Why..."

"Were you there?"

Marvin nodded dumbly.

"O.K.," Big Mike said. "Then stop worrying. It went off just as Johnny planned it. No one else here yet?"

Unger shook his head. He went out into the kitchen and then returned with a partly filled bottle of rye.

His hands still shook as he poured two drinks and handed

one to the big Irishman.

"God!" he said.

"Take it easy, boy," Big Mike said. "It went off perfect."

"I know," Unger said. "But you haven't heard the radio. That horse was killed. Four of the jockeys are in the hospital. There were dozens of people hurt in the riot."

"Yeah," Big Mike said. "And if you listened they also said that the kitty was over two million dollars."

Unger didn't say anything. He lifted the shot glass to his lips and spilled half of the drink getting it down. He started to cough.

"Peatty should be here," Big Mike said. "Hell, they didn't even hold the cashiers. Guess they'll get around to them tomorrow. We all got to get back early tomorrow morning. Everyone who works out at the track."

"How come..."

"Cops just had too damned much to do," Big Mike interrupted. "They picked up probably a couple of hundred suspicious characters at the track. And they're questioning the people who worked in the main offices. They'll get around to the rest of us, don't worry."

"God, I wish it was over," Unger said. "This waiting is driving me crazy. Where the hell are the others, anyway?"

Mike shrugged.

"Take it easy," he said. "Randy has to check out and he didn't want to come direct. He'll be along soon. Peatty should be here, but he probably stopped home to check up on that wife of his. Johnny—well, Johnny has to go back and pick up the loot where Randy dumped it off. He'll be here all right."

"I can't understand why Kennan couldn't have brought it direct," Unger said.

"Don't be a damned fool. You think he wanted to take it in with him when he checked out of the prowl car? For Christ's sake!"

"What happened about the fight?" Unger asked.

"Nothing," Big Mike said. "So far they haven't made the

connection. Killing that horse, that's all they're thinking about right now. And I don't think they've even figured yet what happened to Black Lightning." He stood up suddenly and walked over toward the door.

"Hear the elevator," he said. "Probably one of the boys."

* * * * *

George Peatty was able to get away from the track by seven o'clock. No one had bothered him with questions. They'd only told him to show up the next morning, at ten instead of the usual nine. The cops had their hands full without bothering with the cashiers. Apparently they still hadn't figured out exactly how Johnny had got into the offices in the first place.

George's nervous system was shot and he knew it. But every time he started feeling sorry about ever getting mixed up with the thing in the first place, he'd remember Sherry, And that made it all right.

When he got off the train at Penn Station, instead of going across town and over to the meeting place as he had at first intended, he decided to stop up at his own apartment. For some reason he had been worrying all afternoon about Sherry. He just wanted to stop in and see her, see that she was all right.

He knew, somehow, the minute he put the key into the lock and twisted the doorknob, that something was wrong. He couldn't tell how but he knew.

She wasn't there, but then again, that in itself was nothing to worry about. But this time he did worry. Walking over to the telephone, he looked at it for several minutes. It told him nothing. Then he went through the rest of the apartment. Everything seemed normal. But he still worried. He went back to the phone and he called several of Sherry's friends. No one had seen her that afternoon or evening. He went into the bedroom and opened the top bureau drawer.

George locked the apartment door and went downstairs. He walked over to Broadway and called a cab.

Heading downtown, he felt the bulge where the automatic

weighted down the inside breast pocket of his jacket. His face was yellow and drawn, but his hands were steady.

George had heard at the track that the robbery loot was more than two million dollars.

Johnny had thrown the bag containing the fabulous fortune out of the window. Randy had picked up that bag and driven off. Randy, George knew, was going to transfer the money back to Johnny and Johnny was to bring it to the meet tonight.

For the first time George began to wonder if Kennan actually did transfer the money.

For the first time he speculated on the possibility that Johnny Clay might take that money and light out alone with it.

* * * * *

His mouth set in a tight, hard line and his weak chin was temporarily firm as once more he felt the outline of the revolver.

It was nine o'clock and Randy was talking. Big Mike and George Peatty sat on the couch listening to him as the cop spoke. Marvin Unger paced the floor.

"Sure they know," he said. "They know the dough went out the window. They know that somehow or other it was picked up. So far that's all they do know. They haven't yet connected a police car with it. Whether they do or not, I have no way of telling."

"About you, though," Big Mike asked. "About you? They figure yet you were off your..."

"Yeah. The Lieutenant knows that I didn't answer a couple of calls. But he thinks I got half a load on and was sleeping it off. I'll be busted probably and put back on a beat. But that's all, as far as I know."

Peatty suddenly looked up.

"God damn it," he said, "Where the hell is Johnny? He should be here. What the hell's keeping the son of..."

"Take it easy," Randy said. "Keep your pants on. I dumped the bag all right and Johnny will pick it up all right. He's taking it easy and playing it safe. You don't have to worry about

Johnny."

"I do worry," Peatty said. "How do you know..."

"Look, you little bastard," Randy said, stopping and turning toward him, "don't you get any fancy ideas about Johnny."

"Right, lad," Big Mike said. "You don't have to worry about Johnny."

Marvin Unger stopped his pacing and swung toward the rest of them.

"Well, as far as I'm concerned," he began. And then his voice died out. He turned toward the door. The eyes of the others in the room also suddenly swung toward the door. They had all heard the soft, rustling sound.

* * * * * * *

Johnny Clay left the newsreel theater at seven-thirty. He had seen the program through and then sat on for half of the second showing. Once more he was feeling all right. It was almost like coming out of a post-operational shock.

He walked across town, taking his time. When he arrived at the parking lot on West Fifty-first Street, the place was rapidly beginning to fill with the theater crowds from the suburbs. He waved the attendant who approached him aside, and went to the office.

"I'm a friend of Randy Kennan's," he said. "Supposed to pick up his car. He tell you about it?"

The man at the desk looked at him for a second, and then smiled.

"Sure," he said. "Sure thing. You know the car?"

"Yeah."

"It's the Dodge sedan—the blue one, second row over at the end," the man said. "Key's in it. You want to go down and take it out yourself? The boys are kinda busy right now."

Johnny said that he'd take it out.

"Any charges?" he asked.

"No, he keeps it here by the month," the man said.

Johnny thanked him and walked out.

It felt strange driving again.

Joe Piano opened the iron grilled door in the basement when he rang the bell. He said nothing until after Johnny was in and he had started following him down the hallway.

"He came," he said then.

"Good."

"Yeah, he came and he left it. It's up in your room."

"Thanks," Johnny said.

He followed Johnny to the door of his room.

Johnny started to unlock the door.

"You won't be back, I guess?"

Johnny went into the room and then turned and closed the door after Joe Piano followed him in.

"No," he said, "1 won't be back." He hesitated a moment, his eye taking in the duffel bag laying over in the corner.

"I'd like to do something for Patsy," he said.

Joe Piano shook his head.

"You don't have to," he said. "You already done enough."

"I'm going to leave something for Patsy in the bureau draw-er," Johnny said.

Piano stared at him for a minute.

"O.K.," he said. "You can do that then. I'll tell him." He turned and reached for the door knob.

"Some stick-up out at the track this afternoon," he said. A moment later and he was through the door and was closing it softly.

Johnny went over to the duffel bag. He opened the draw cord and put one hand in, pulling out a sheaf of bills. He didn't bother to count the money but went to the bureau drawer and opened it. He shoved the bills inside and then closed the drawer.

A moment later and he closed the top of the duffel bag and threw it over his shoulder. He carried it downstairs.

Joe Piano was waiting at the iron gate and opened it for him.

"I left the key on the bed," Johnny said.

"Good luck," Joe said. "I'll tell the boy what you did for

him."

Johnny went to the car at the curb and tossed the duffel bag over the door so that it landed on the floor next to the driver's seat. He climbed in and pushed the starter.

* * * * *

Val Cannon stopped the car in front of the apartment house and cut the lights. He turned and spoke over his shoulder.

"Get the key out of her bag," he said.

The thin-faced man reached down to the floor and picked up the leather strapped, woman's pocketbook. He fumbled around inside and finally took out three keys on a small silver ring.

"Must be one a these."

"Ask her," Val said.

The heavy-set man laughed.

"Ask her hell," he said. "She's passed out again."

"O.K. Get her ass off that seat and carry her inside. You pass anybody, say she's drunk. Take her upstairs and dump her."

"You want we should try and bring her to?" the thin-faced man asked.

"I want you should get her inside her apartment and drop her." Val turned into the back of the car. "And God damn it, get back down here right away. You've had your fun with her. I want to get on downtown."

The big man carried her and the thin-faced man opened the doors. Entering the apartment, the smaller man flipped on the light switch at the side of the door.

The other man dropped Sherry Peatty on the couch in the living room. He turned away.

His partner walked over and looked down at her for a minute.

He lifted his hand and slapped her twice across the mouth. She didn't move. Deliberately, he spit into her face, then turned away.

"Dumb bitch," he said.

Val had the engine going as they both climbed into the front seat. Twenty-five minutes later he pulled up in front of Marvin Unger's apartment house. He cut his lights and as he did a man stepped out of a car across the street and walked over. He leaned on the side of the door.

"Well?"

"The guy got in shortly after six," the man said. "The big Irishman came in around eight-thirty, then the other guy who works at the track and the cop soon after."

"How about…"

"No. He hasn't showed. Of course he could have got here before I did, but I doubt it."

"O.K., Trig," Val said, at the same time reaching for the ignition key and taking it out. "We're going on up. You stay down here and wait. If he's already up there—fine. But I doubt it. If he should show, I want you to give him plenty of time to get inside and upstairs and then follow him on up. I'll see you."

He turned to the others.

"You all set, Tiny?" he asked.

The heavy-shouldered man grunted.

"You, Jimmy?"

"Couldn't be more set," the smaller man said. He shifted in the seat and loosened the gun in its shoulder holster.

"Let's go then," Val said, opening the door on his side of the car.

* * * * *

Randy Kennan was reaching, almost instinctively, for the gun he always carried as the door burst open. He was standing not more than three feet away and the big man's blackjack caught him across the eyes before he had a chance to move.

Val followed the big man into the room and Jimmy shut the door quickly behind them.

Unger, Big Mike and Peatty stood frozen.

Randy Kennan slowly slumped and then sprawled on the rug. Blood began to seep from his nose and down across his chin.

"All right," Val said. "Just hold it. Don't nobody make a move."

The gun was in his hand and he stood with his back to the closed door. The heavy-set one, the one he had called Tiny, stood balancing on the balls of his feet, gently moving the blackjack back and forth. Instantly the thin man went into the bedroom. He returned a moment later.

"No one else," he said.

Val nodded.

"Get that slob on the couch and take his gun," he said.

The other two lifted Randy to the couch, at the same time frisking him. Kennan opened his eyes and stared at them.

"The rest of you sit down."

Peatty slumped into a chair near the kitchen. Unger, his face deadly pale, leaned against the edge of the couch. Big Mike just stood for a second. His face was red as a beet.

"I said sit down."

Mike went over and sat on the couch next to where Randy was slowly trying to get up. He put a hand on Randy's knee and held him down.

"Search the joint," Val said.

There wasn't a sound then as Tiny and Jimmy started going through the place. It took them only two or three minutes.

"Nothing," Jimmy said, finally returning from the bathroom. "It ain't here yet."

Val nodded. He turned to Unger.

"All right, you bastard," he said. "When do you expect him?"

"Expect who?"

Val didn't answer. He walked across the room and using the barrel of the gun, swiped it across Unger's forehead, leaving a wide red gash which quickly filled with blood. Unger half sobbed and sat down on the floor.

"I'll ask the questions. When do you expect him?" Val turned to George Peatty.

"We don't expect anyone," George said.

Val walked over in front of him.

"You're cute too," he said. This time he used the butt. Deliberately he smashed it into Peatty's face.

"Two down and one to go," he said as Peatty fell from the chair to the floor. He turned to Big Mike then.

"O.K., Papa," he said. "We know all about it. We know you guys knocked off the track. We know you're splitting it up, here, tonight. And we're cutting in. Now when does that other son of a bitch show up here with the money?"

Big Mike looked at him for a moment before speaking.

"He don't," he said then. "We were just getting set to meet him."

Val started toward him, again holding the gun by the butt. As he did, Randy suddenly kicked out and caught him with a blow on the shins. At the same time he rolled off the couch and started to reach for the blackjack he carried in his hip pocket. Tiny's own blackjack caught him across the top of the head as Val stumbled and fell over him.

Unger screamed.

It was then that Peatty fired.

The bullet caught Val Cannon in the throat and he suddenly coughed and the blood began to pour down his shirt. Big Mike leaped for Tiny and at the same instant Jimmy began shooting. His first shot hit Marvin Unger in the chest.

The second one entered George Peatty's right cheek.

Big Mike, backed against the wall in a bear hug, hit the electric switch. A moment later the place was in complete darkness.

And then hell broke loose.

* * * * *

Mrs. Jennie Kolsky, sitting in her living room in her apartment directly under Marvin Unger's, got up and walked over to the telephone.

"I don't care what you say, Harry," she said, "they got no right making all that noise over our head. Like it or not, I'm calling the police."

She picked up the receiver and dialed for the operator.

Five minutes after she had put the receiver back, Mrs. Kolsky was in her bathroom, washing her face with cold water. She was nervous and it always calmed her to wash her face. It wasn't often that Mrs. Kolsky had found it necessary to call the police department.

Lifting her face from the washbasin, she reached for a hand towel. She was looking directly into the mirror.

That's how she happened to see the face.

The blood-soaked face of the man who was making his way, fumbling blindly, down the fire escape which showed through the opened window opposite the mirror over the sink.

Mrs. Kolsky screamed and the sound of the scream suddenly blended with the sirens from the street below.

❈CHAPTER XI❈

The wail of the siren reached Johnny Clay's ears at exactly the moment he caught sight of the flashing red light in the rear vision mirror over the windshield.

It took iron nerves, but he carefully slowed down and pulled over to the right curb of Third Avenue. He sat there then, hardly daring to breathe, as the speeding police car came up to him and a second later passed in a wailing scream of sound.

The car swung to the left a block beyond and turned into East Thirty-first Street.

Johnny knew.

He knew just as well as he knew he was driving that blue sedan on Saturday evening in the last week of July.

He didn't hesitate, but followed the car around the corner.

The police had stopped in front of the apartment house.

Johnny didn't hesitate, nor did he speed up. He drove past the parked car and kept on going. Halfway down the block he passed the dimly silhouetted figure of a man staggering in the shadows of a tall building. He glanced at him only casually.

Ten minutes later he found the secondhand store on the Bowery. He pulled up at the curb and went in. When he came out he was carrying two light weight suitcases.

It took time, but he finally found the dark deserted street out near Flushing. It was difficult in the dark, but still it didn't take more than ten minutes to transfer the money from the duffel bag to the two suitcases. When he was finished, he tossed the bag into a clump of bushes and put the suitcases on the floor at his feet. He backed away and headed back toward the Parkway.

He tried the radio but was unable to get a news program. Looking at his watch, he saw that it was just eleven o'clock.

A mile from the airport, he again turned off the boulevard. He found an all night restaurant not far away. He knew that he would have to kill another twenty minutes. He pulled up in front of the place, shut off the ignition and went in and ordered a cup of coffee.

Leaving the restaurant ten minutes later, he saw a newsstand across the street. He went over and bought an early edition of the next morning's tabloid newspaper. He didn't bother to look at it, but folded it once and put it into his side coat pocket. And then he started for the airport.

* * * * *

The driver had looked worried when he had climbed into the back of the cab.

"You sure you're all right, Buddy?" he asked.

"Yeah—all right," George Peatty mumbled. "Just a nose bleed. Bad nose bleed," he said. He sounded drunk.

"Where to then, Mister?"

It was then that the thought hit him. He knew that he was badly hurt, he knew that he wasn't quite clear in his head. But also, at that exact moment he remembered. He remembered the airline brochure which had fallen out of Johnny Clay's pocket three nights before, the last time they had all met at Marvin Unger's. He remembered now. It had been bothering him all along, and now he remembered.

"La Guardia," he said in a barely audible voice, "La Guardia Field."

He reached into his trouser pocket and took out several bills which he had neatly folded twice. Carefully, moving almost like a man in a slow motion picture, he peeled off the top bill and handed it through the window to the driver. It was a tenspot.

"Stop somewhere and get me a box of kleenex," he said.

Somewhere near the tunnel he must have lost consciousness because he couldn't remember getting over to the Island. By the time the lights of the field were visible, he knew that he couldn't last much longer. He was having a hard time seeing and it took all of his will power to focus his eyes, even for a minute.

But he had to get away.

He couldn't go home. They'd be looking for him at home.

* * * * *

Fay Christie looked at the clock over the information booth and then checked it with her watch. Her watch was right. It was just ten minutes before midnight.

God, she didn't think it would be like this.

Why didn't he come? Where was he? What could have happened?

And then, again, she struggled to control herself. The plane left at half past twelve. He'd said midnight. He'd said that without fail he'd be there at midnight exactly.

Nervously she stood up and started toward the restaurant. But then, once more, she hesitated. She doubted if it would be physically possible for her to swallow another cup of coffee.

Five minutes later she again got up. Slowly she started walking toward the doors leading out to the taxi platform.

She had to move aside as the man staggered through the doors and past her. He looked drunk and he was holding a handful of kleenex to his face. His clothes were badly stained and it looked as though his face had been bleeding.

The man almost staggered into her as she moved out of his way. His eyes were wide open and they had an odd, blind look about them.

And then she saw Johnny.

A small, half sob escaped from her throat and she ran toward him.

He dropped the suitcases and he was holding his arms out to her.

"Johnny—oh, Johnny!"

She was half crying.

She buried her face in the collar of his coat.

Johnny's hand reached up and he caressed her head. He started to say something to her, looking down at her as she began to lift her face.

Neither of them saw George Peatty. Neither of them saw the gun in his hand.

George's voice sounded as though he were drunk as he mumbled the words. The blood was pouring from his mouth as he spoke and it was almost impossible to understand him.

"God damn you, Sherry," he said. "So you're running away with him, are you."

He pushed Fay away from Johnny as he spoke.

"You can't," he said. "You can't."

And then the revolver began to leap in his hand.

The bullets made a peculiar dull, plopping sound as they followed one after the other into Johnny Clay's stomach.

* * * * *

The matron held the smelling salts under her nose and turned her own head away. She looked up at the airline hostess who was hovering over the two of them.

"Poor darling," she said. "I guess the sight of blood was too much for her. It's certainly taking her some time to snap out of it."

The airline hostess nodded.

"You don't suppose she could have known him, do you?" she asked.

Fay Christie opened her eyes and looked around her blankly for a second. And then, without having made a sound, the tears began to well up and roll down her cheeks.

Out in the lobby the uniformed policeman leaned over and pulled the blood soaked newspaper from under Johnny Clay's elbow.

"Keep those god damned people back," he said.

His eyes fell on the headline and unconsciously it registered on his brain.

RACE TRACK BANDIT MAKES CLEAN BREAK
WITH TWO MILLION.

CPSIA information can be obtained at www.ICGtesting.com
Printed in the USA
BVOW01s1602230913

331854BV00003B/38/P